TH DROWNING MAN

It all began because he wanted to write a bestseller; it ended with blackmail and double-cross, intrigue and murder, and a desperate fight for survival.

Tony Blake had come to interview low-life Private Investigator Ronnie Elliott, but within days the PI was dead and Blake was embroiled up to his freshly scrubbed author's neck in a real-life murder mystery.

Having adopted, almost by default, the persona of his own fictional character, Richard Mahoney, he has no choice but to delve deeper into the seamy, violent underbelly of the sleepy, down-at-heel northern seaside town.

One step behind him are the sour and jaded local cops, Walker and O'Neal, in front of him are the lowlife thugs of the underworld and scheming entrepreneurs.

On the positive side he discovers a willing, friendly and more than accommodating sidekick in the curvaceous form of Mandy Woodall, and has to resist the advances and not inconsiderable charms of his client 'employer' the mysterious and dangerous Helen Fitzsimmons.

Like a *Drowning Man*, Tony Blake, aka Richard Mahoney, gambles with his credibility and his life in pursuit of the truth behind a series of seemingly random deaths and innocuous incidents. But with the events unfolding around him taking on a momentum of their own, time is running out . . .

THE
DROWNING
MAN

Gary Mortimer

GREAT NORTHERN PUBLISHING

THE DROWNING MAN

ISBN: 1 9037100 0 6

First published by Great Northern Publishing 2002
in association with Gary Mortimer.
All rights reserved.

~

GREAT NORTHERN PUBLISHING
'The home of quality publishing in Yorkshire'
PO Box 202, Scarborough, North Yorkshire. YO11 3GE
books@greatnorthernpublishing.co.uk
www.greatnorthernpublishing.co.uk

Designed and typeset in 10pt Aldine by Great Northern Publishing (Services).
Approximate word count: 64,000 words.

Printed and bound by
Bookcraft (UK)

DEDICATION

This book is dedicated to my family and friends for their support and encouragement as we travelled in Mahoney's wake.

For the doubters, of which there were one or two (you know who you are), read it and weep!

About The Author

Born in 1959, Gary attended Scalby School with the intention of becoming either a professional footballer or a rock star; he spent much of his time watching re-runs of old 1930s and 40s 'films noirs' starring the likes of Bogart, Cagney and Bacall, with the result that he became neither. In an attempt to make up for his lost youth he achieved an Honours Degree and an MA in Writing at Sheffield Hallam University, before gaining a PGCE Certificate at Bretton Hall. During successful teacher training placements at Colne Valley and Rawthorpe High School, he wrote a weekly sports column for a local paper, and was joint editor of the critically acclaimed journal *The Titanic*.

Gary has spent numerous summers silver-spoon-feeding rich American children at Timber Lake Camp in New York, and despite having spent the last six years as a dogsbody for the Civil Service, his sense of humour and ambition has never waned. When not interviewing for the Camp America programme, the author is busy working on the sequel to this, his debut novel.

He would like to thank everyone who has contributed to this novel in some form or other; in particular his mum, dad and sister; Rosie Hartless; Carol Procter; Richard Tyroler; Susan Willcox; Nigel 'how bizarre' Keatley; Wendy McPhee; Matthew Savage; the staff at Yorkshire Coast College; Mark Marsay at Great Northern Publishing; and Jeff 'where's me dinner?' Taylor for his constant criticism - he wouldn't be where he is today without it, and neither would Gary.

1

Reluctantly, the train pulled into the heart of Scarborough. Actually it wasn't so much a heart, more of a blood clot; hardly a sprawling, soaring monster with a steel skeleton and a concrete overcoat, more a sinking, sulking menace with a brittle backbone and a borrowed raincoat.

I'd been to Scarborough before. It's one of those things you do, like jumping off a high wall or sticking your finger into a socket, and it has much the same effect - you never want to do it again. Even the tide thinks twice about coming back.

Out beyond the cold stone platform and the cold stone walls stood an endless line of traffic lights stuck on red. The station clock showed three different times and the people didn't appear to have moved an inch since my last visit; there were the same young girls pushing prams because they didn't want to be left on the shelf and the same young men running from bookies to bars drinking themselves into that age-old dream that maybe things will turn out better next week. Just the names had changed.

A couple of leafless trees squeezed out from the uneven pavement and there wasn't the slightest hint of soft sandy beaches. No brightly coloured posters. No welcoming guest houses. Nothing at all to suggest I'd just set foot in one of the country's top seaside resorts. For all I knew I could have landed on the moon.

My memories were of days on the beach playing football and nights in the loud, neon-lit arcades saving the earth from space invaders. In truth, there hadn't been a whole lot else to do. And when it had rained people had huddled in shop doorways with a bag of chips and scribbled hasty 'wish you were here' postcards to anyone and everyone.

Those days might have gone but I still had a sense of dread as I picked up my bag and headed down main street.

~

Ronnie Elliott's office was a two-minute walk from the station. He'd been offered a place in the middle of town, amidst the other 'thriving' businesses, but times had been hard and it was clear that the town no longer thrived. Vacancy signs littered the dirt-stained windows of discarded guest houses and B&Bs, the trees in the parks had withered and died, and the rickety old church across the square mournfully rotted away under the weight of abject neglect.

I pressed the bell to Elliott's office. Nothing happened, so I pushed open the door. It opened on a large, damp hallway with pale yellow walls and bare, creaky floorboards. A woman in blue overalls was meticulously sweeping the stairs. She hadn't heard me enter, or if she had she didn't give a damn. My shadow stretched out across the floor and up the stairs in front of her, making her jump. She spun on her heel.

"Shit! You scared the life out of me!"

"Sorry," I muttered. "I was looking for Ronnie Elliott's office."

She looked at me as if she felt she should know me from somewhere. Her hair was short, white, and tinged with the tell-tale yellow stain of nicotine addiction. Her lips were thin and red and they didn't move a whole lot when she spoke.

"First floor," she said, pointing up the stairs. "On the left."

"Thanks."

The stairs moaned under my weight, and the smell of furniture polish and stale fags hung in the air. There were two doors on the landing. The one on my right had a frosted glass panel with M. WOODHALL ~ QUANTITY SURVEYOR printed on it in gold leaf. The door opposite had a large wooden frame with a dirty grey undercoat that was chipped and scraped. The letters R. ELLIOTT PRIVAT INVEST OR had been stuck to the plain glass.

I tapped on the door. It squeaked slowly open. I craned my neck and peered inside. "Mr Elliott?"

There was no answer. I shoved open the door and stepped inside.

The office was small and cramped. They say you can tell a lot about someone simply by the place they inhabit. Well, the two chairs, tall grey filing cabinet, two-seater leather couch, large wooden desk with a 'No Smoking' sign, telephone, sink with a dripping tap, shelf stacked with razors, pair of ill-matched stained mugs and three blue gambling chips probably said all there was to say about Mr Ronnie Elliott.

I shuffled through the paperwork scattered across the desk, mainly bills. A creased copy of the *Sun* lay open at the racing pages. Ronnie had been busy: the names of six horses were circled in blue.

The air was dark and damp. Droplets of dust danced in front of the short, grey curtains that had been drawn to mask the afternoon glare. They matched the worn grey carpet that rippled like a fading tide across the floor. A raincoat was slumped across the back of a chair.

I strolled to the window and pulled back the curtains. It was a clear day and when I stood on tip-toe I could see about an inch of sea pressed tight between the bright blue sky and the dull grey seagull shit on the rooftops below. But there was no sign of Ronnie.

Back at the desk I decided to write a note, just to say I'd called. I was still searching for a pen that worked when the door flew open and a short, stocky pair of grey trousers shuffled into the room. The man wearing them had his head down and was struggling to do up his flies.

He looked up startled when he sensed he had company. He was sweating profusely and breathing heavily. Thin strands of brown hair stuck to his head, 'Bobby Charlton' style. He gave me a cold, 'Who the hell are you?' stare.

I looked back with, 'I hope he's got the wrong room.'

"If you've come for the money, you're out of luck. So get lost!" he snarled.

"Money?"

He finished doing up his flies and kicked at the door with his heel. It shuddered to a close and another letter fell to the floor. Pretty soon Ronnie was going to become a 'VAT INVEST OR'.

As the little man drew near I found myself transfixed by his multi-coloured tank-top pulled tight over a bright yellow shirt with a collar wide enough to fly a plane. The turn-ups on his trousers were hunched up over dirty white trainers that must have seen better days.

"My name's Tony Blake." I said. "I'm a friend of Eddie's."

The furrow in his frown was deep enough to plant seeds.

"Eddie?"

"Yeah, Eddie Hargreaves . . . your brother-in-law!"

"Oh yeah," he said, without enthusiasm. He took a deep breath and heaved his trousers up and over his pot belly.

"So. Are you . . . Ronnie Elliott?" I was praying he'd say no.

"That's what it says on the door, doesn't it?"

"Actually it says 'Privat Investor'. Or at least it did when I came in."

He was standing so close to me I could smell his rank breath. It was like he hadn't cleaned his teeth for weeks.

"A clever dick, eh?"

I wanted to say yes, but not in the sense that he had perhaps intended, so I shook my head apologetically and looked away from the glare of his tank-top.

"Blake?" he mumbled, as if reluctant to recall some not too distant and painful memory. "Oh yeah, I remember, you're the bloke writing a book!"

He made his way over to the sink and splashed water over his face a couple of times, then looked up at the mirror and patted a few loose strands of hair back into place.

"So what're you doing here?"

The question took me by surprise. "What do you mean?"

"Well, in case you haven't noticed, this isn't a library!"

"Didn't Eddie tell you?"

"If he did I've forgotten. I can't remember everything people tell me!"

That was promising, a Private Investigator with the memory of a goldfish. I imagined him three days into a case suddenly wondering what the hell he was supposed to be investigating.

"I'm writing a story about a PI. Richard Mahoney."

"Never heard of him!"

"I made him up."

Elliott fixed me with his gaze. "Is that what you are . . . a Private Dick?"

"No! I just write about them."

"What for?"

I shrugged my shoulders. "Nothing better to do, I guess."

Elliott lowered his gaze and went back to towelling his face. "And I suppose you think it's a life of fast cars, sun-kissed beaches and busty blondes?"

"No," I said, "they don't all have to be blonde!"

I watched as Elliott draped the towel over the sink and moved to pull the curtains closed. The whole place suddenly went dark. He carried the frown back to his desk and sat looking at me for a moment.

"So what's all this got to do with me?" he asked eventually.

"Well I . . . like I said, I'm not a detective and I've never done anything like this before, so I'm a bit short of ideas. That's why Eddie suggested I should come and see you."

He twisted his face this way and that and wrapped his hands round the back of his neck. I couldn't help noticing the patches of sweat under his arms.

"Well I hate to spoil your fun, young fella, but you've come to the wrong place if you're looking for inspiration."

"Actually, I just need some ideas that's all."

Elliott got to his feet and moved to fill the kettle. "You're still wasting your time. You see, this isn't some big city place like London or New York. This is a poxy little seaside town with poxy little people who do nothing but complain about their poxy little lives and how nothing ever happens here. There's a football ground up the road but the closest they ever get to a riot is if they forget to let folk out at half-time. Actually, I tell a lie, two reporters got into a fight last week over who should cover the cat getting stuck in a tree headline!"

Elliott was getting a kick out of this. There was a glint in his eye like the first of his six horses had just come in.

"What about you?" I asked.

"What do you mean?"

"You must get by."

"So?" he snapped.

"So, what do you do?"

For a moment he didn't say a word. He just looked at me with a pained expression and went on looking till I didn't think he was ever going to stop. Then he wiped his nose on his sleeve and replied, "Legal advice mainly. There's never any murders or anything like that. The only time I get out of this place is when I'm hired to find some disillusioned kid who's gone and got himself even more disillusioned somewhere else."

He held up a mug. I nodded.

"Have you always worked here?"

"No, I spent a couple of years down in the smoke."

"London?"

"London, Birmingham, Glasgow, it's all the same; too many people who don't give a damn."

I started to circle the room.

"I guess that's what being a Private Investigator is all about, young fella, a load of cheating and mistreating. People who don't know they're born and people who wish they hadn't been."

What I could still make out of the sun had sunk behind a large black cloud. The office was cold but that's how I figured Ronnie would have liked it. Anything else would have had added a human touch.

"Pity Eddie didn't tell me sooner, I could have saved you a journey."

The kettle shrilled and Elliott disappeared in a cloud of steam as he filled the mugs.

I was still circling the room as he placed the mugs on the desk along with an almost empty packet of digestives. He offered me a sympathetic smile. It didn't help.

"If it's all the same to you, I'd like to stick around anyway!"

He held up his hands like it didn't bother him one way or the other.

I picked up the mug and sipped at the tea. It was horrible. Everything about Ronnie Elliott was horrible.

"Do you live alone?" I asked.

He took a swig of tea, most of which trickled down his chin. He wiped the dregs off with his sleeve, all the while looking at me with a 'what the hell's that got to do with anything?' expression.

"It's just that most hard-boiled PIs do!" I said.

"What am I, an egg all of a sudden?"

I shook my head and smiled. An egg would have more personality.

"It's an expression. Hard-boiled PIs are tough, thick skinned. They have to be in order to survive."

Elliott smiled like the survivor he obviously thought he was.

"Usually they live alone. It's this notion that they can solve everybody else's problems but their own."

"And what makes you think I've got problems?" he growled.

"Doesn't everybody?"

He banged his mug onto the desk and reached for a handful of paper.

"These are my only problems, young fella," he said, waving a fistful of bills in the air. "But as long as people can't help themselves then I'll be all right, if you know what I mean."

I looked at the bills and I looked at Ronnie and while I tried to think of what to say next the phone rang. It startled us both.

Elliott snatched it up and yelled "Yeah?" into the receiver.

He didn't seem to like whoever it was. But then again, maybe that was just his manner. The caller did most of the talking while Elliott stabbed nervously at the desk with a pen and kept glancing over at me like he wished I'd up and disappear.

Things were growing heated. "Yeah. Look, I said I'd be there, didn't I? So I'll be there. Right . . . yeah . . . right."

He slammed the phone down and sat staring down at the floor for a few seconds. Then he got to his feet. "I've got to go."

"Can I come?" I asked quickly.

"No! This is personal . . . I mean it's my dad, he needs some things."

"Will you be back?"

Elliott checked his watch, shook it, then asked me the time.

"Three-forty-five."

He nodded. "I doubt it."

"What time do you start in the morning?"

He shrugged. "Nine. Ten. Not much to do once I've read the papers."

Elliott dropped a hat onto his head. It didn't do him any favours. At the door he began fumbling through pockets. I shuddered to think what he might find there. Eventually he came up with a key and threw it in my direction. I caught it one-handed and looked back at him.

"Key to the office," he explained. "If you get here before I do, put the kettle on. Might as well make yourself useful. In the meantime I'll try to find you a dead body."

Elliott left the office laughing.

I looked at the key in my hand. It seemed a nice gesture considering he hardly knew me. But then, there wasn't a whole lot to hide. At worst I could run off with his bills, at best he'd have a cup of tea waiting for him in the morning.

I slipped the key into a pocket, wandered across to the window and pulled back the curtain. Outside the sky had turned a heavy, overcast grey. Pretty soon people would be huddled into shop doorways, eating chips and scribbling 'wish you were here' postcards to anyone and everyone.

~

With nothing to do and nowhere to go I took a walk. I hadn't planned on coming all this way just to sit and stare at four office walls and listen to a tap drip all night.

Outside the rain had ceased, leaving behind damp pavements and sporadic puddles. The sky was clear, and at first I couldn't see a single star, but, as with problems, the longer I looked the more I saw until it was as if every star in the galaxy was on show.

I took a right turn into a cul-de-sac where two large Victorian-style hotels stood, set apart by a circle of parked cars and a square yard of grass. Each displayed enticing photos of sumptious bedrooms and crumb-free lounges. All I had was twenty quid. I turned away. I had been hoping that Ronnie's hospitality would stretch to a cup of coffee and a sofa at least. But that had been before I'd met him and realised he wasn't the kind of man who enjoyed handing out gifts.

The choice was mine. I could either treat myself to one night in a sumptious room with a crumb-free breakfast and head for home the next day. Or I could grab myself a takeaway and slum it in the office for a few nights until Ronnie's bad breath and the dripping tap drove me away. Not much of a choice . . . but it was all I had.

~

I unlocked the office door and dumped a brown paper bag onto the desk. I filled and plugged in the battered, scaled-up kettle and reached for the jar of coffee. It was empty. There were no tea bags either. I found it hard not to hate everything about Ronnie Elliott.

I searched the filing cabinet. The first drawer had some files with client details and nothing else. The second drawer held a box of sharpened pencils, a pencil sharpener and some more paper. I pulled open the bottom drawer and a bottle rolled into view. I picked it up. Whisky . . . and it was full.

I hated whisky. I'd only tasted it once but that was enough never to want to try it again.

I picked up the framed photo lying discarded in the drawer. It was a picture of Ronnie, his arm around the shoulder of an older man sitting in a wheelchair. Ronnie was smiling, but he didn't look happy.

I left the photo and went back to the desk with the files and the whisky. I wondered why it was such a popular drink with PIs. Was it simply a vice, an opportunity to forget? Or was it a means of separating themselves from the troubled world in which they lived?

Storm clouds gathered outside the window as out in the distance a tiny trawler dipped and climbed across the heaving waves. I sat and ate. I was starving, but the burger simply disintegrated in my mouth. It was nothing like the one in picture above the counter; you'd have needed a week to eat that.

The files didn't reveal much. There were names and addresses. A couple wanted Ronnie to investigate a lawsuit. A man wanted him to tail his wife who he thought was having an affair. The rest were accompanied by passport-sized photos of people wearing the same haunted expression. It was as if it was the first time they'd ever looked into a camera. All were young. All were missing. And all were searching for something they couldn't find here at home.

I poured some whisky into a mug and sipped. It tasted as I remembered, and stuck to the back of my throat, gradually setting fire to my lungs. I hated it, but figured it might get me through the night.

Outside 'cats and dogs' rained down on the dark, depressing streets. The stars had disappeared, but it didn't mean they were gone. My eyes searched the office. It was hard to believe that all Ronnie had to show for fifteen years of poking his nose into other people's affairs were a few photographs, a sink with a dripping tap and a bottle of whisky. A bottle which was rapidly emptying . . .

I finished the food before I finished the whisky. My breath stank and my eyes were growing heavy. The room looked more appealing by the second. All I needed now was the hypnotic fragrance of a beautiful woman sitting cross-legged on the edge of the desk. And I wasn't fussy, Lauren Bacall would have done just fine, as long as she came with a case of money and a face that looked good on my pillow.

My head felt like a sponge, my eyelids had shut as tight as vault doors and the walls had closed in around me. Sometime tomorrow the Brighouse and Rastrick would be playing inside my skull. It would be a tune I'd recognise, but it would be a tune that I'd never want to hear again for as long as I lived.

~

I was cold and in pain. It felt like my head had been squashed into a matchbox and run over by a truck. If I wasn't dead I should have been. A shrill ringing pierced my brain and refused to let me rest in peace.

The morning light sliced into my eyes as I gently forced them open. I tried hard to focus on a chair, a window, a door, anything that wasn't strapped to the carousel I seemed to be riding on. Nothing looked right. Everything was sideways.

A fist twice the size of my skull banged away inside my head as I sat up, slowly, and watched a desktop unfold before me. An untidy desktop littered with fast-food leftovers and a half-empty bottle of whisky.

I cradled the pain in the palm of my hands and suddenly realised where the ringing was coming from. I snatched at the phone and yelled "Yeah?"

I could hear a voice, but it was very faint.

"Look, this is a bad line, you'll have to speak up!" I snapped irritably. Then realised I had the receiver upside down.

I turned it round.

"Is Mr Elliott there?" The woman's voice cut through my head like a knife.

"Er, no. No, I'm afraid he isn't. Can I help?"

"Well, perhaps I could leave a message?"

"Yes, of course," I said, holding the phone at arm's length and scrambling for a pen.

"Ask Mr Elliott to meet me in Il Ristorante."

"Il what?!"

"Il Ristorante. The Italian on Queen's Avenue. I have a table booked for seven-thirty. Have you got that?"

"Yes," I said, scribbling, 'Ristorante' and 'seven-thirty' across the racing page of yesterday's paper.

"And make sure you tell him it's of the utmost importance that I speak with him."

"Yes. Right. And you are?"

"I'm sorry?"

"Who shall I say called?"

"Helen Fitzsimmons," she replied, like I should have known all along. "And please . . ."

"Yes?"

"Tell him not to be late!"

Tell him not to be late! She'd be lucky if he was there at all. Where the hell was he anyway? He'd said nine, or ten, and it was gone eleven. This might be the first decent case he'd had in months and there was no sign of him.

I got to my feet far too quickly and the fist started banging away inside my head again. I should have said he was ill, or on holiday, or something.

I searched the desk for his home number. I found it on an invoice and dialled. There was no answer.

I tried to think of what to do next, but the thumping grew louder, preventing me from thinking about anything other than removing my head with an axe. With all the grace of a blind man walking on broken glass I crossed to the sink and turned on the tap. It was loud, too loud. I let the cold water run and then held my face under water for as long as possible. It didn't clear my head but the tingling sensation numbed the pain for a while.

I towelled myself down and headed out into the hallway. The cleaning lady was outside humming the kind of tune that only she'd recognise.

"Excuse me." I said, quietly.

She turned and smiled, obviously relieved to find I wasn't in the habit of scaring her to death every time we met.

"Have you seen Ronnie this morning. Ronnie Elliott?"

She shook her head. "Have you tried Spillanes?"

"Spillanes?"

"Yes, it's a wine bar."

I checked my watch. "But it's only eleven-thirty!"

"He likes the food."

Why didn't that surprise me?

"And the music."

But that did.

"Is it far?"

She shook her head again. "It's in the middle of town. You can't miss it."

But she didn't know me. Right now I could miss a barn door if it was nailed to my face. I was only two hours into a three-week hangover. I needed sleep. There was a pillow out there somewhere with my name written on it, a dream waiting to happen with me on some tropical island surrounded by coconuts and bikinis.

What I didn't need was a wine bar filled with loud music and a crowd of people.

2

It took me half an hour to find Spillanes: a dingy wine bar that disappeared off the high street down a hundred narrow steps. The place was hardly humming, there were just a few people propped on bar stools or leant against the bright lilac walls. Across the smoke-filled room a man and woman took to the stage. The man looked like he'd been dragged off the street. He wore a tight fitting T-shirt, turned-up jeans and trainers. His hair was thick, but hadn't been combed in weeks. The woman was thin, with coal-black hair and grey streaks. Or was it grey hair dyed black? It was hard to tell from where I stood. They looked like the kind of people who'd given up on fame and fortune a long, long time ago . . . but boy could they play.

He plucked the guitar strings like his soul depended on it, and she had a voice that made my toes curl. They were singing the blues and that's a dangerous thing when you're alone in a bar nursing a hangover.

But nobody else was listening. They either laughed or talked and then put their hands together when the song ended.

I looked around. There was no sign of Ronnie.

I decided to hang about and pulled up a stool close to the door. It seemed like as good a place as any to sit and wait.

A barmaid raised her head at me. This was obviously some kind of sign that came from working in a place where nobody could be heard. My brain still felt like it was trapped inside a spin dryer but there's this thing I have about walking into a bar and not ordering a drink.

"Pint of bitter, please."

The girl was offended at having to talk. I'd upset her routine.

"We don't serve beer."

She had all the charm of a pit bull that had missed breakfast.

"So what do you do?" I asked.

"What?"

"What do you do?"

"Wine!"

"So I've noticed, but what have you got to drink?"

She handed me a list. It was full of cocktails and fancy wines I'd never heard of; exotic drinks from all over the world, and probably all brewed up the A64 in Tadcaster.

I ordered an Elephant, it was the only thing I could pronounce. She gave me a bottle and a glass - they didn't serve pints. I left the glass on the counter and sipped straight from the bottle. The Elephant tasted just like that, thick, grey and heavy. It slid down my throat and bounced into my stomach like a rubber ball falling down a dry well.

"Why would you come to a wine bar and order a pint of bitter?"

The voice was a summer breeze, soft and warm with just the faint hint of a hot, sticky night ahead. It belonged to the pair of large brown eyes sitting next to me. I would have described the rest of her but I was lost in those eyes.

"I've never been to a bar that didn't serve beer."

"You've never been in here before then!"

"Maybe I have. Maybe I haven't. And maybe I've just got a terrible memory."

Her smile was smooth, like silk. The corners of her mouth stretched just enough to spark a twinkle in her eye. Her hair was short and blonde and smelt of coconuts and I couldn't help wondering what she would look like in a bikini.

There was a confident air about her, the way her whole body was turned towards me. I have two words for women who get this close to me, short and sighted.

She studied me closely for a minute. "No. I can definitely say I've never seen you in here before."

"Do you remember everyone you see?"

"Only the interesting ones."

I took another drink and tried to contain the hormones that were ready to reach out and greet her with open arms.

"My name's Mandy, by the way."

"Tony. Tony Blake."

She smiled.

"And why are you drinking alone, Tony Blake?"

"I'm er, I'm waiting for someone," I stumbled.

She appeared put out.

"A man, actually," I clarified quickly. And realised how that sounded. "A Private Investigator, man, I mean."

"A Private Investigator man!"

I nodded.

"Are you in some kind of trouble?" She sounded concerned.

I laughed and said no, as Mandy sipped her drink. It was clear and packed with ice. She turned to look at me, a strand of hair hanging loose in front of her eyes. She flicked it back into place and said, "So what's his name?"

"Ronnie Elliott. Do you know him?"

She straightened her back and nodded. "As a matter of fact I do. He comes in here quite often. But I haven't seen him today."

I looked at her and smiled, checked my watch and saw the minutes ticking by.

"Would you like me to give him a message . . . if I see him that is."

I turned and found her staring straight at me.

"If you like."

"Anything in particular?"

"Just that he's supposed to be meeting someone."

"A client?"

I looked back at her without answering.

"And what if I don't see him?" she asked.

"Then you won't have to tell him anything, will you?"

"I was thinking about your client."

"I didn't say it was a client!"

She smiled. "And so this, someone . . . what exactly are you going to tell them if you don't find Mr Elliott?"

She was looking at me over the top of her glass and I couldn't help thinking that she asked a lot of questions. When I didn't answer she looked upset.

"I was only trying to help."

"All right, she's a client," I said, eventually. "But to be honest I don't know what to do if Ronnie doesn't show."

"Why don't you cancel the appointment?"

"I don't have her number."

She pressed her glass close to her cheek and looked out across the room deep in thought. She took her time in speaking again, almost as if she enjoyed the chance to ponder what to say next.

"Is it important?"

"It could be."

"Then go in his place."

The idea first intrigued me and then made me laugh. "She asked for him by name."

"Mmm . . . then tell her you're his partner."

"He hasn't got a partner."

"Does she know that?"

Mandy was staring at me. She knew she held all the aces. I picked up my drink, forgetting how foul it tasted. Everything she said made sense, but maybe that was because I liked what I'd heard and I liked who'd said it.

She stretched out a hand and gripped my arm. Her fingers tightened as she whispered in my ear, "From the moment I saw you I thought you were a Private Investigator."

And while I waited for the punch line the ice melted in her glass. "You did?"

She nodded.

"Well . . . I . . ."

She pressed a painted fingernail to my lips.

"All you have to do is ask her what she wants you to do. It might be nothing at all, but if I know Ronnie, he'll be very grateful to you."

But she couldn't have known Ronnie, not that well anyway. I'd only known him five minutes and already it was obvious he couldn't spell gratitude, let alone feel it.

"It's up to you of course," she continued, slowly inching herself off the stool and looking me deep in the eye. "But what have you got to lose?"

~

I went back to the office and thought about what Mandy had said. I thought about it a lot and most of it made sense.

The smell of stale food and Ronnie's cheap aftershave still lingered. I opened a window and the noise from the street burst in with the early evening fog.

Hanging from a nail above the sink was a mirror. It was a head and shoulders fit. I pulled on my ear like Bogart in *The Big Sleep*.

"From the moment I first saw you I thought you were a Private Investigator."

"This is stupid. I don't know the first thing about being a PI. All I've ever done is read books and watch films," I told myself.

It was five-thirty. I dialled Ronnie's home number and let it ring.

There was still no answer.

"All you have to do is talk to her . . ."

Perhaps I was making too big a deal out of nothing. Perhaps I could say that Ronnie's sorry but he's busy on another case.

No! Because she'd think her case wasn't important enough for him to handle himself.

Maybe I could tell her that he was ill and that I was a friend . . . partner, Tony Blake.

"Tell her you're his partner."

I couldn't. I just couldn't . . .

What remained of the whisky was making eyes at me. I put down the phone and poured myself a glass. It still tasted vile, but it made me think.

If Tony Blake couldn't meet with Helen Fitzsimmons, then maybe Richard Mahoney, PI could. He was cool and sharp. He was a hero waiting to happen . . .

I picked up the raincoat still slumped across the chair and put it on. It was a pretty good fit. Ronnie had obviously outgrown it and it felt good. I felt complete. Batman came with a cape, Wonderwoman came with two large eyes, and PIs come with a raincoat.

In the gathering gloom I raised the glass to 'Richard Mahoney, PI, a man willing to sacrifice everything in search of the truth, a detective who refused to be soiled by the corrupt world that surrounded him, a man prepared to be beaten to a pulp and dumped by every beautiful girl that came into his life . . . and that was on a good day!'

3

I arrived at the restaurant a few minutes early. Tiny white candles glittered through soft pink curtains giving the place a warm, rich presence. Warm I liked, rich I could do without.

Il Ristorante was, by reputation at least, one of the town's more exclusive establishments. You didn't go there for the food, or the immaculate service, you went there to be seen. It was expensive, and it was 'in'. ·

I was greeted by a thin man with a very irritating high-pitched voice. He curled his lip as he asked, "Can I help you . . . sir?"

"Yeah, I'm looking for Helen Fitzsimmons."

"Is she expecting you?"

I looked down at the bushy eyebrows and the thin moustache. I didn't like him. I wanted to say something low and meaningful. I wanted to wipe the snot-nosed expression off his face. But I was here on business, not pleasure.

"Yeah. She is."

He ducked his head into his shoulders a couple of times and ran a scrawny finger along the inside of his collar.

"I'll show you to a table."

He wasn't happy. He didn't like people like me blotting his landscape.

He could smell money a mile off and I didn't even whiff.

It wasn't busy, but that didn't stop him hurrying me to a secluded table. Out of sight, out of mind. He left me with a menu big enough to change behind.

~

Helen Fitzsimmons was ten minutes late. It had taken me just ten seconds to realise I couldn't afford anything on the glossy, overpriced menu. For the other nine minutes and fifty seconds I sat and waited.

She was not what I'd been expecting. The waiter greeted her from across the room like she was some Hollywood movie star.

Every face in the room was transfixed by the way she breezed in.

She walked like women don't any more, her hips swaying to the gentle tap of her heels. The glint in her eyes suggested she was enjoying every second of the attention she held with a finger-click. All that was missing was the smooth sound of a sax accompanying her across the floor.

"Mr Elliott?" she purred as she held out a hand across the table. "I'm so glad you could make it."

I held on to it like it was a valuable piece of china.

"Actually . . . I'm afraid Ronnie couldn't make it."

"Oh!" she said, taking back her hand with alarming speed, eyeing me suspiciously.

"He's ill . . ."

She appeared lost for words. I tried to seize the initiative.

"He asked me to come along instead. I'm . . . I'm his partner, Richard. Richard Mahoney."

She sat down cautiously and looked me up and down.

"That's odd," she said. "I had no idea Mr Elliott had a partner."

The remark drifted off into silence as I sat down and began nervously rearranging cutlery.

"I . . . I didn't realise you knew him," I managed, eventually.

"I don't."

"So, what made you think he didn't have a partner?"

"Because his was the only name advertised in the telephone directory."

I tried to hide my relief, but it wasn't easy now that I had three knives and just the one spoon on the table in front of me.

"Well . . . er, that's because I work out of Manchester. I'm a friend of a friend, so to speak. I'm just helping him out, as a favour kind of . . . until he gets better. I wasn't really expecting to be doing much."

She raised an inquisitive eyebrow.

"I mean, I thought people came to the seaside to get away from their problems!"

"Perhaps some people are just born unlucky," she said quietly.

I acknowledged her observation with a subtle smile while the waiter shuffled over with a notepad and pen.

She picked up a menu. "What would you like, Mr Mahoney?"

"Something I can spell!" I frowned.

She smiled. "Are you not at all hungry?"

"Not at all."

"A coffee perhaps? I insist you have something."

"I think I can manage a coffee."

"Two coffees please, Simon."

Simon wasn't happy. He'd calculated his percentage of the coffees and realised it wouldn't even cover his bus fare home.

Helen Fitzsimmons sat upright in her chair. "You know, you don't look the least bit like a Private Investigator."

"Oh! And what exactly do Private Investigators look like?"

The return of Simon with our coffees forced her to remain silent. He placed a tray on the table and laid out the cups and saucers. Then he mumbled something under his breath and rearranged my cutlery. I was too busy watching Helen Fitzsimmons to care. I was trying to read her, but it wasn't easy. Her face gave little away. Her eyes were pale blue. Her lips full and sensuous. Her teeth pearly white. Her hair was brown and cropped, every strand perfectly ordered and in its place. Only the thread of dark cotton hanging from the shoulder of her well tailored jacket was out of place, something brave enough to intrude on her perfect world.

Simon slipped the bill into a leather, gold-embossed folder and hurried away.

Helen Fitzsimmons stood and slid her jacket off with well-practised grace as if she knew people would be watching her every move. Then she sat back down and leaned confidently across the table to me.

"Well," she began, "whenever I've had to deal with Private Investigators in the past, I've found them to be rather aloof, faceless creatures. Their only concern is how much money they're going to make." She paused to sip her coffee, leaving me to ponder on which side of aloof I was about to fall. "You, on the other hand, appear more like one of those Private Investigators one sees so often on the television."

"You mean six inches tall?"

"I mean," she said, abruptly, "that I feel I can trust you. That you will get the job done, quickly and effectively, and that you won't go selling my deepest secrets to the highest bidder."

I dropped two lumps of sugar into my cup and then remembered I was meant to be cutting down. Not that I was fat - far from it. But a single man in his thirties needs to hang on to all the shape he's got.

"So, is that why I'm here? Are you about to reveal your deepest secrets?"

She didn't answer. Instead she reached into her bag and pulled out a pack of cigarettes. She offered me one, but I declined, even though I was sure Mahoney would have enjoyed a smoke from time to time.

"Tell me, Mr Mahoney," she said, disappearing behind a cloud of blue-grey smoke, "why have you been following me?"

The question took me by surprise. Completely.

She dropped the dead match into the ashtray and glanced at me with a cute smile, the kind of smile children give their mother when they're about to ask for extra pocket money.

"Following you?"

"Oh come now, Mr Mahoney, don't play games with me."

Her tone was confident. It went with her eyes.

What the hell had Ronnie been up to?

"I didn't know I was," I said, with more honesty than she would ever know.

"Well, Mr Elliott, your partner, has, and not very effectively at that!"

"Been following you?"

She nodded.

"And how would you know that?"

"Because he's been asking the most impertinent questions and sticking his nose in where it doesn't belong."

"Mind telling me where exactly?"

"In my business affairs."

"And why would he want to do that?"

"I was rather hoping you would tell me!"

"Well, like I said, I've only just met him."

"Then perhaps you can give him some advice."

"And what's that?"

"Tell him to keep away . . . for his own sake, as well as yours."

It sounded like a threat and she looked like she meant it. She pushed her cup across the table, stubbed out the cigarette and stood up. She was ready to leave, but I wasn't in the mood to let her. I didn't like carrying the can for something I hadn't done and I didn't want to go back to the office and pass my time reading files on missing children and drinking what was left of the whisky.

I took her hand. "Look, I said I work with Ronnie, not for him. If you've got a gripe with him that's fine, but don't take it out on me."

She looked at me like I'd slipped an ice cube down her blouse.

"Now why don't you sit down and tell me what's really on your mind?"

A hush had fallen over the restaurant. Everybody was looking in our direction and it was making Helen Fitzsimmons feel uncomfortable. She forced a smile to her lips and sat back down.

"I was right, wasn't I? You're not at all like all those other PIs."

Simon returned to fill our cups.

"Is everything all right, Mrs Fitzsimmons?" he mumbled, nervously.

"Yes." She looked straight at me and took out another cigarette.

"So," I began, "if Ronnie's following you it's because somebody's paying him to. Have you any idea who?"

She blew a ring of smoke and nodded. "Somebody I used to know."

"Let me guess, some old flame you haven't yet extinguished?"

It was obvious she hadn't been prepared to go this far by the way she squirmed and avoided meeting my eyes. I got the feeling she'd just wanted to put the brakes on Ronnie and would have been satisfied with that. The trouble was, I wasn't Ronnie.

"Not exactly," she said softly. "I think it's my husband, Colin."

"Your husband?"

"Yes. But only in name. We separated a year ago. Why we ever got together in the first place I'll never know."

"And now all of a sudden he wants you followed?"

She took another long pull on her cigarette. "Have you ever heard of Roger Laughton?"

It was a rhetorical question. Laughton owned half of Scarborough, the half with all the money in it. Every hotel and restaurant you stepped into had his name on it - even this one.

I nodded. "Yeah. Why'd you ask?"

"He's my father."

"I'm impressed."

But Helen Fitzsimmons wasn't flattered. She offered me the Bette Davis hurt kind of look and toyed with her cup, her long, elegant, perfectly manicured fingers turning it this way and that.

"I thought you might be. Most people are . . . even Colin finally woke up to the idea that he'd married a fortune. What he didn't realise is that my father and I don't exactly see eye to eye. I'm independent, Mr Mahoney. I like to take care of myself, but that wasn't enough for Colin, he had big ideas."

"But that doesn't explain why he should want you followed."

"My father is about to retire. He doesn't want to of course, he's a proud man but the doctors have told him he doesn't have a choice. And if I know Colin, he's already assumed he's entitled to half of the business."

"Is he?"

"Over my dead body! Colin is a waster, a dreamer. He purchased a second-hand record shop with the bright idea of creating a nationwide chain. Five years later all he has is a second-hand record shop. A poor one at that . . ."

"Perhaps he's looking for an angle to squeeze in on your old man's business?"

She rolled her eyes as she tried to make sense out of what I'd just said.

"I think I understand what you're suggesting."

"So what do you want from me?"

"A favour?"

I sipped my coffee and considered the word 'favour' carefully. Mahoney wouldn't like it very much, because it sounded like 'voluntary', something you might enjoy if you were an honest-to-God Christian, or a good cop, or both.

"I'd like you to follow Colin. Find out exactly what he gets up to."

I sat back and admired Mrs Fitzsimmons' confidence. It came from someone who assumed everybody had their price. How rude! How obvious! How much?

She stubbed out her cigarette, dipped a hand into her bag and fished out a photograph, a head and shoulders shot of a man straining a smile at the camera.

I was about to pick it up when she took hold of my hand.

"His shop is on North Avenue, the name escapes me for the moment."

"And all I have to do is follow him?"

"Yes. Take note of who he meets and what he gets up to. Anything at all."

"Then what do I do . . . whistle?"

"I own a couple of shops, one on the Foreshore Road, the other in the precinct at the top end of town, you can reach me at either."

She placed an envelope on the table. It was open and I could see a stack of notes, a lot of notes. My heart skipped a beat.

"Consider this an appetiser, Mr Mahoney."

And while my mind drifted to thoughts of sun-kissed beaches filled with coconuts and bikini-clad babes she stood, slipped on her coat, noticed the cotton thread hanging from her shoulder and with a strange look of satisfaction plucked it up and let it fall to the floor. She raised an eyebrow in my direction.

"Do as I ask and I guarantee you'll enjoy the main course."

Every eye was fixed on her as she left the room.

I picked up the photo and gave it one last look. Colin Fitzsimmons appeared flat and featureless. He was somewhere in his mid-thirties, a man trapped between what he wanted to be and what he'd become. He had a wide nose and cauliflower ears that stuck out a mile. It was hard to imagine Helen Fitzsimmons offering him so much as a second glance let alone marrying him. I tucked the picture into my pocket, and while everybody else got back to eating and talking, I finished my coffee and contemplated the storm that had just swept into my life and wondered if a raincoat would be all the protection I'd need.

4

Following Colin Fitzsimmons was going to prove difficult. The bus station at the top of town was now a deserted lot where yesterday's headlines gathered under broken windows and where kids played on skateboards. So hopping on a bus every time he made a move was out of the question. I needed a set of wheels of my own.

A man in a flashy suit wrapped an arm across my shoulders and led me around his showroom as if I was some long lost friend. Perhaps he was deceived by my suit and tie. He patiently went into detail about every fancy car on display until I told him how much I actually wanted to spend and that I was only looking to rent something for a couple of days. Suddenly he remembered an important call he had to make back in the office and left me with a young man scratching his bum and rinsing out his shammy.

Five minutes later I left with a pale blue Ford Fiesta. It wasn't exactly what I'd had in mind, and by that I mean it wasn't a Buick Roadmaster, but at least it didn't stretch too far into the money Helen Fitzsimmons had handed me.

I drove back to town. I was tired.

That night in the office with a desk for a pillow still had me pulling splinters from my face. I needed a treat. I drove down Columbus Avenue. It was as I'd remembered it when I'd stayed there with my parents. Every street in every seaside resort should look so good. Wide, clean and quiet, with small neat gardens, trees that marked the edge of the pavement and guest houses with colourful hanging baskets and names like Derwentdale and The Dolphin.

I pulled up outside the first one I came to with a 'Vacancy' sign in the window.

The open door led me into a hallway laid with a carpet so thick it was like walking on air. A hat stand and coat rack stood to my left and a large mirror reflected my gaunt features back at me. I pulled on my ear - I even looked the part. Mahoney would be proud of me I told myself.

Soft, welcoming music rose from behind the tall reception desk. I hit the obligatory bell and stood back to scan through a list of 'What to do in Scarborough'. It took me all of three seconds. For children, water slides and amusement parks abounded. For the elderly there were gardens and 'summer' shows featuring entertainers who only came here to retire but who had been wheeled out for one last show.

Next to a poster of two hideously ugly stand-up comedians was a small sign advertising the local Writers' Circle. The chairman was a local author called Ms J. Simms, and they were meeting later that night.

I convinced myself it wouldn't be a complete waste of time to mix with other 'creative types'. It was amazing what wearing a raincoat and renting a car had done for my confidence.

Eventually a large, plump woman with rosy cheeks appeared before me. She wore a flowery purple dress held together with a flowery apron. Her smile was warm and sincere. She looked like the kind of hostess you could wake at four in the morning and ask for a bacon sandwich and she'd smile sweetly and say it would be no trouble at all.

She wheezed as she spoke. "Can I help you?"

"Yes. I'd like a room please."

She looked momentarily surprised, as if holidaymakers were a thing of the past.

"You are open?"

"Certainly," she smiled, deftly opening the register and reaching for a pen. "And how many nights would it be for?"

Good question! How many nights was I planning to follow Colin Fitzsimmons?

"Maybe I could just book a couple, and then I'll get back to you. I mean, it could be more." It could be a whole lot more.

She introduced herself as Barbara and led me upstairs to the first floor. The room was small and clean. A wardrobe, TV and single bed all encased in lilac wallpaper. Barbara was proud of her establishment and proud of the fact that the street had yet to succumb to the 'giro ghetto' as she termed it. She said it was important to know that there were still parts of town that readied themselves for the occasional holidaymaker, instead of the all year round security of a dole cheque.

I dumped my bag on the bed and she asked if there was anything else I needed. I said no, and she handed me a key and asked me to mind my noise after eleven o'clock on account of her regulars. I nodded, smiled and watched her leave.

It didn't take me long to 'unpack' two pairs of trousers, three shirts, a camera, an assortment of underwear, socks and a bristle-battered toothbrush. Already bored I flicked on the TV, but there wasn't much of interest. All the sporting events had been cancelled because of the bad weather and the schedule was taken up with repeats of seventies American dramas that hadn't been worth watching first time round.

It was only five-thirty, but I was ready to throw myself at the tender, inviting mercy of the bed. I needed all the sleep I could get. But I also needed food and the creative inspiration of the Writers' Circle.

~

The taste of salt and vinegar lingered on my fingers as I entered the library. I couldn't help thinking there was something slightly unsettling about holding a Writers' Circle meeting above a library. I'd always thought of them as a kind of graveyard for books. After all the hard work of writing, applying, begging, rejecting, publishing and selling, this was where they were finally laid to rest and dusted down from time to time, if they were lucky.

I followed the directions up a flight of stairs and into a room decorated with posters advertising plays by Ayckbourn and Shakespeare, and novels by Bronte and Hardy. The thought of a novel starring gumshoe Richard Mahoney paled into insignificance against such literary giants.

The tables were gathered into a small horseshoe in the middle of the room and six curious faces turned and looked up at me simultaneously as I entered. Some were old, some middle-aged. None of them seemed particularly pleased to see me.

"Is this the Writers' Circle?" I asked nervously.

A woman stood up and smiled. "Yes. Have you come to join us? Please, do take a chair."

I was careful not to sit next to anybody. People tended to want their own space, especially where strangers were concerned.

Ms Simms introduced herself and then quickly introduced everybody else. I instantly forgot their names. The atmosphere was weird and probably not a million miles away from an AA meeting.

Pretty soon I felt I'd be getting to my feet and introducing myself as Tony Blake, a thirty-six-year-old nobody with a fixation on a fictional character I would dearly love to be in real life, who sleeps in an office and drives a pale blue Fiesta.

"Now," Ms Simms smiled. "I believe we were just about to hear how Gerald's getting on with his work. Gerald."

Gerald was a tall man. He could have changed a light bulb without rising from his chair. His shoulders were round and hunched. He cradled a piece of paper in penny-pinching fingers. He spoke through thin lips and clenched teeth, trying hard not to give too much away. He informed the group he'd written a short story about a garden shed. It was a metaphoric shed, and everything in it stood for some, less than fascinating, aspect of his life.

My suspicions were quickly realised as it soon became apparent just how boring Gerald really was. He had a deep whining tone that stretched every word into about fifteen syllables.

So it was that my mind found itself wandering off around the room, exploring. It began with Ms Simms, a woman of about forty-five. She wore a long flowing dress and just a hint of make-up. She had a nervous laugh that completed her every sentence and made me wonder just how sincere she really was. She sat through the entire evening staring at everybody from beady eyes with a grin that suggested, that whilst her body was there, her mind was elsewhere liaising with giant mushrooms and sticking flowers in her hair.

There was a small poster on the wall behind her advertising a novel she'd written, 'Emotionally Attached'. I figured it was probably some feminist stab on the failings of man (or men in general).

Next to Ms Simms, with an ever-present frown, was a young woman called Sophie, or Sandra, or something like that. She was from Australia, the land so full of promise that everybody leaves it to fulfil their potential everywhere else. She hung limpet-like on every word that issued forth from Ms Simms' lips.

Then there was Trish. Trish with the long brown hair, high cheekbones and a smile that I knew would stay with me long after bedtime. She wore a short tartan skirt and black leggings and I wondered if she was seeing anyone.

But that was wrong. I was meant to be concentrating on my novel and I knew full well that PIs (the good ones at any rate) never got involved with women, especially beautiful women with high cheekbones. It was Chandler's golden rule, women represented the corrupt society that

Marlowe was meant to absolve.

I tried to turn my attention back to Gerald who was rabbiting on again, "Dirt . . . worm . . . business associate . . . receivers . . ."

I stifled a yawn.

Sophie nodded and began humming.

I suspected Ms Simms was as bored as I was and was perhaps singing every Dylan song ever recorded over and over in her head.

And Trish . . . with the high cheekbones, black leggings, and legs crossed at the ankles. Maybe it was time to bend the golden rule . . .

Eventually the sun closed its eyes, the evening drew to a convenient close and everybody packed away their pens and inspiration, such as it was. Ms Simms sat at the front of the room talking to Trish. It seemed like a good opportunity to be introduced. I sidled up to them and waited for Ms Simms to smile.

"So, what did you think?"

"Yes, it was OK."

"We like to spend time on one particular piece of work, we find it's more beneficial that way, don't we, Trish."

Trish nodded.

"Have you met Trish?"

"No," I said.

I looked at Trish and offered her my warmest smile. It was supposed to make me look sincere but always appeared as if I'd just had all my teeth filled.

She smiled back, but didn't say a word. It just made her more appealing. Silence is power I thought, and right now she was Wonderwoman.

"So you'll come again?" Ms Simms assumed.

"Sure."

"We have another meeting on Thursday, you're quite welcome to come along. Or you can join us in the pub. Most people are on their way now for a quick drink, nothing like a drop of alcohol to set the critical tongues wagging."

Ms Simms slapped the desk and laughed like she'd never laughed before.

"Yes, I'd love to."

~

The bar was quiet and we sat at a table in the corner of the room. For a while I stared up at the walls. They were decorated with sepia photos of the town taken in days gone by, when trade was booming, the place was clean and everybody was happy. Which is more than could be said for those at the table. There were no distinctive characters. No jokers telling tales. Everyone was politically correct and uptight. They spoke of the brilliance of Morrison and the tackiness of Archer and I thought, yeah, but he's a million seller, and who the hell are you?

There was no sign of Trish.

I was finishing my pint when Gerald turned his long limbs towards me and asked about my novel. I gave him a brief description, but as usual I did myself no favours as I stumbled over words and phrases fresh out of the mangle. He asked if I'd read any Agatha Christie. At first I thought he was being polite, in the way someone might comment on the weather, or my health. But no, he was sincere.

Christie was the only crime author he'd ever read and therefore he wasn't sure if he'd be much help when it came time for the group to discuss my work. I smiled politely and saw Chandler turning in his grave at the thought of Agatha Christie being mentioned in the same breath as classic crime novels. I didn't like Poirot. He came across as such a snob, someone whose only approach to crime was to wait until all the murders had been committed and then point his stubby Belgian finger at the last person left standing.

"No, I haven't," I answered politely.

"Oh."

And that was that. The evening went as flat as my beer. I decided it was time to say goodnight to Tony Blake, the nobody author, and hope that tomorrow the sun would bring a fresh and exciting dawn for Private Investigator, Richard Mahoney.

5

At nine o'clock on Monday morning I pulled up across the street from Colin Fitzsimmons' record shop. That was my first mistake. He didn't open until ten.

I tried calling Ronnie again, but there was no answer. It crossed my mind to call the police, but I hardly knew the man. Maybe he did this kind of thing all the time. Maybe he was off chasing after some disillusioned kid who'd become even more disillusioned in London or Birmingham. And then again, maybe I didn't care. Maybe I didn't mind how long he stayed away, because maybe I was enjoying playing the big cheese.

There was a secluded spot across the road from the shop. I pulled in and sat unnoticed watching the shop, and the large billboard displaying the kind of scantily-clad girl you only ever saw on billboards. She was spread like butter on a golden beach, surrounded by palm trees, sipping an ice-cold drink. The billboard suggested we get away from it all. Out on the streets the town shuddered into life, the beat of heels and the chugging of cars its anaemic, sluggish life-blood as people hurried to jobs they couldn't wait to leave.

At nine forty-six a small maroon car breezed into the street and pulled up outside the shop. Fitzsimmons, looking every inch like the man in the photo only now complete with arms and legs, stepped out and strolled to the newsagent's next door to buy a paper. I aimed the camera and took a few trial shots. I was rusty.

Through the lens I got a clear view of the shop. I could make out the details of the window display of rare posters and faded album covers. On the door were plastered adverts for local bands and music lessons.

At ten precisely the lights flickered on inside the shop and the 'CLOSED' sign flipped to 'OPEN'. I sat wondering what to do next.

Fitzsimmons crossed the floor and started to arrange a stack of records he was holding in the window.

Helen Fitzsimmons only wanted me to follow him, no more. And she was the one paying the bills.

At five, after a long and uneventful day, the lights went out and the 'OPEN' sign was reversed. Nothing had happened. Nothing at all. Customers had come and gone, students mainly, and middle-aged men dressed in black T-shirts and denim jackets. I saw only two people buy anything. Nothing to write home about, and certainly nothing to bother my client with.

I took another three snaps of Fitzsimmons as he locked up, then started the engine and pulled out into the commuter traffic. I trailed him three cars back.

It turned out he lived in the 'old town', down by the harbour, on a street recently renovated with neat little apartment blocks. He pulled up outside number twenty-two, locked the car and went inside. I saw a light go on and it stayed on until a little after eleven. Then a light went on upstairs and the curtains were drawn.

Ten minutes later the light went out.

I checked my watch. It was almost eleven-fifteen and I was starving. I needed food. Fitzsimmons wouldn't be going anywhere, not until morning. Unfortunately there was nowhere open - Scarborough had closed for the night. I glanced back at number twenty-two and envied

Fitzsimmons tucked up in bed while I was outside in the cold; tired and hungry. Being a PI wasn't quite as romantic as I'd first thought.

~

It was much the same the next day, Tuesday, and that bothered me. I could have set my watch by the street's routine, and my car was piled high with unfinished puzzles and fast-food leftovers that had begun to attract the attention of a couple of neighbourhood strays.

My first ever case had developed all the appeal of a Hermit's Tea Party.

Halfway through the day I decided to take a break from pizza and burgers and treat myself to something more substantial. I was already putting on weight and I feared that if the 'stakeout' went on for much longer I'd end up being trapped inside the car for the rest of my miserable life.

There was a bakery-cafe on the corner. It gave off the sweet and inviting smell of freshly baked pastry. Girls in bright yellow uniforms and matching hats wiped their brows and busied themselves behind the counter. I took my turn in the queue and eyed the menu.

"Er, a cheese and salad sandwich, please."

The girl went off and came back a moment later smiling. "Sorry, we're out of cheese."

I stared up at the board. "But it's there, in black and white," I moaned.

"We're running down."

"You've run out? But it's only two o'clock!"

"No," she smiled sweetly, "we're running down."

I was confused.

"If we put too much on it just goes to waste."

"And of course you wouldn't want to risk selling too much!"

But the girl had charm and wasn't going to let my tantrum rattle her. She stood smiling at me and there was nothing I could say or do. I was hungry. I couldn't get what I wanted. And she was all sweetness and light.

"How about an egg mayonnaise then?"

"White or brown?"

"Anything, I don't care, just as long as I can eat it now."

Back outside the traffic had come to a standstill. Drivers tapped their steering wheels and tried to stay calm amidst the annoying choruses of "Are we there yet, Dad?" and "I told you it was left back there!"

The truth was they were only yards from the beach, but the town was equipped with a transport system that snared travellers in a web of one-way streets that took bewildered drivers anywhere and everywhere but where they wanted to be.

There was no escape. They dared not turn tail and head home for fear of a series of major road-works controlled by men in brightly-coloured vests who leant on shovels and scratched their heads and arses wondering where the giant hole they were protecting had suddenly come from.

It was a simple yet effective way of ensuring that once the tourists had arrived they were here to stay. At least until they'd spent every last penny they had brought with them.

I finished the sandwich and walked a hundred yards to the nearest bin. Stretching my stiff back, I stared across at Fitzsimmons' shop and decided it was time to meet the man face to face. I could buy some tapes, they'd provide a welcome change to the constant drone of the local radio in the car.

The door eased open as I stepped inside. Fitzsimmons sat on a stool behind the counter, smoking a pipe and reading a tattered paperback. He lowered his head and studied me over the top of his dark-rimmed glasses.

"Hi."

He curled his lips into a faint smile and went back to his book. I viewed the shop. It was small and cramped, and it smelled of smoke and plastic dust covers. There were browser racks on either wall, stuffed with every kind of album imaginable. If you wanted it, it was there. A range of CDs and cassettes were stored in glass cases. On the floor in a corner was a cardboard box crammed with old 45s.

A shaft of light slipped in through the window and picked out the dust dancing across the room like gently falling snowflakes. I felt like I was standing inside one of those 'snowstorm' paperweights. Music played. It sounded like Springsteen on a bad day, and I'd never known him to have a good one.

I crossed to the rows of tapes.

Marlowe enjoyed classical music but I don't know Brahms from Liszt, so I settled on a collection of classics and headed to the counter. Fitzsimmons got to his feet. He was about five eight with long mousy hair that fell in waves over his shoulders. He looked tired, his face was thin and pale, with a poorly cultivated goatee stuck to his chin, probably for effect, but why? And for whose benefit? He moved slowly, without disturbing his vague expression. He took the tape and wrapped it in a paper bag. I handed him the cash and watched him open the till.

I was studying him so closely he looked at me and frowned.

"Sorry," I mumbled. "It's just that you remind me of someone. I've been out of town a while and I have a problem trying to fit names to faces."

"Colin Fitzsimmons," he muttered, handing me the tape.

"Colin Fitzsimmons!" I nodded. "That's right, aren't you married to Helen?"

He studied me for a moment. "Yes. Why?"

"Oh, no reason. Like I say, I'm just trying to put names to faces. So how is she?"

"We're separated," he said softly.

"Oh, I'm sorry. I didn't know," I mumbled. "So you don't see her any more?"

"Like I said, we're separated."

If ever I'd wasted ten minutes of my life it was there in that shop. He had all the charm of a German tourist hogging the poolside loungers. Perhaps I'd asked the wrong questions. Perhaps I hadn't asked any 'leading' questions. Perhaps being a PI was going to be a lot harder than I thought.

I took the tape back to the car and hoped I'd never have to speak to Colin Fitzsimmons again.

6

Fortunately events took a turn for the better the next day. I'd packed some sandwiches for a start, and I was getting into the new tape, Handel's Water Music; so appropriate considering the rain crashing down on the windscreen.

At five o'clock Fitzsimmons shut up shop and I started the car. I needn't have bothered. After buying an evening paper, he hurried down the street, collar turned up against the cold and rain. I sighed, got out and followed him to a small cafe. He sat at a corner table alone, lit his pipe and ordered a drink.

I sat and waited until a girl in a pink blouse and tea-stained apron shuffled across to me. She was spinning gum around her mouth and talking at the same time.

"What can I get you?"

"Coffee."

She wrote it down like she might forget by the time she reached the kitchen. "Anything else?"

"No thanks."

She tucked the pad into her apron and shuffled back to the counter, passing empty cups and discarded plates en route. It was then I realised what it was I liked about the town: the pace. Or rather, the lack of it. While the rest of the civilised world spun wildly round in one direction, Scarborough toiled against the tide in the other.

I watched Fitzsimmons drink his tea and check his watch with monotonous regularity. Perhaps he was waiting for something, or someone.

The waitress returned with the coffee, most of it in the saucer. She stepped back and appraised me with large 'go ahead punk' eyes.

I smiled and said, "Thanks."

It took all of thirty seconds for the lumps of sugar to disappear through the thick treacly froth. By which time Fitzsimmons was heading for the door.

I stood up quickly and followed him out, back into the rain.

He drove slowly along the foreshore towards the lighthouse. The rain eased up and then stopped. Darkness had fallen with a thump, and a big heavy dish of a moon hung low on the horizon. Stars littered the sky like crystals and a row of streetlamps arched out over the road, their yellow beams dancing on the tranquil waters.

Fitzsimmons took a right, onto the pier, and drove up to the lighthouse. I stopped twenty yards away and waited. And waited. My watch ticked around to six thirty and still I waited. Fitzsimmons hadn't moved. He just sat there in his car flicking through the evening paper whilst seagulls swooped across the bay, waiting impatiently for the return of the fishing boats.

I wound down the window and tried to relax to the sound of the waves kissing up against the harbour wall just as another car drove onto the pier. It stopped beside Fitzsimmons. Immediately he got out of his car and leant against the railings. A figure climbed out of the other car, a female figure. The night was cold and dark and she was dressed for it. Her heels clicked across the cobbles as she made her way over to Fitzsimmons. I brushed aside the stack of empty pizza boxes on the passenger seat and grabbed the camera.

The pair didn't stay very long, and Fitzsimmons appeared to do most of the talking, waving his arms around a lot. The woman stared out across the sea, as if waiting for her ship to come in.

I was halfway through a roll of film when she turned and headed back to her car. Fitzsimmons stayed long enough to watch her leave.

It was 'fun' while it lasted, but it hadn't lasted long enough. All too soon I was back outside number twenty-two, watching the lights go on as I huddled inside a blanket trying to stave off the cold.

I turned on the radio for a change, but all I could get was the local station. It was dire. Ad-jingle singers sang of carpet sales and furniture bargains as if their hearts had just been broken. And the DJ kept telling me how lucky I was to be listening to his show. I was about to go back to my tape when he introduced a guest, a lady by the name of Betty Cummins, the local UFO expert. She sounded convincing. She'd devoted her life to looking for strange lights in the sky, tramping across vast expanses of the lonely moors at the dead of night. I imagined her with a like-minded group all dressed in X File T-shirts with Star Trek intercoms. It was only a matter of time, Betty assured listeners, before contact was made.

I didn't have the heart to ring and ask why 'intelligent' beings from another planet would want to visit Scarborough, they'd have to queue all day on the A64 and there'd be no food left in the shops when they eventually arrived.

For perhaps twenty minutes I stared at the downstairs light, wondering if the mystery woman might turn up. Who was she? Fitzsimmons' lover? Perhaps they'd been planning a rendezvous. But why go to so much trouble? Why not talk on the phone? And why hadn't they kissed or even embraced?

I had the sudden urge to urinate. It must have been all the tea I'd been drinking. I couldn't recall Marlowe ever having gone to the toilet. He daren't. He might have missed something important. I might. Perhaps his bladder control only served to emphasise just how superhuman he was. I didn't know and it didn't help wondering about it. I wasn't superhuman. I was from Manchester and now I had a bladder the size of a football.

I crossed my legs and hoped the woman wouldn't turn up.

At twelve forty-five the lights went out and I was alone with my thoughts. Ten minutes later I assured myself Fitzsimmons was fast asleep and that nothing was going to happen. Down a dark, lonely alley relief came flooding out.

7

The 'old town' was a warren of small, tight-knit cobbled streets. I chose one at random and walked between tidy red-roofed fishermen's cottages with freshly scrubbed doorsteps and colourful hanging baskets, perched precariously on the edge of the castle hill. I emerged on the foreshore and stood for a moment, lost in the shadows that leapt up from the gift shops and amusement arcades.

The bay was quiet. Only the ghosts of fishermen's tales rose from the tranquil waters and the nearby inns where once they would have regaled each other with their great adventures.

Spring was looming and the promise of long, sunny days was in the air.

The beach was empty, its wet surface stretching like glass towards the waves where only seagulls dared paddle. Donkeys huddled together and pressed their faces into sacks of oats and a lonely figure hurried to tie a tarpaulin over the stacks of unused deckchairs as a dull mist crept in from the sea. So much for spring.

I turned my collar up and wandered to the first of Helen Fitzsimmons' shops, close to the Foreshore Theatre. A gaggle of tourists draped in overcoats and scarves frowned at the names on a hoarding. They were gradually realising the town only attracted those long past-it entertainers who chose to associate themselves with once glorious, but now fading seaside resorts.

The shop was called The Treasure Chest - how original - and was packed with every novelty imaginable; tea towels, rock, postcards, sunglasses, mugs, pictures, caps; nearly all of it tacky and inexpensive, emblazoned with scenes of the ruined castle or the less than splendid Spa. A youngster, fresh from school, with a face and spots to match, was busy rearranging plastic models of the castle and talking to a couple of browsing customers.

He told me Mrs Fitzsimmons was out, but was due at the other shop in about an hour. He offered to draw directions on a scrap of paper, but I told him I'd have no problem finding it. He smiled and asked if I'd be interested in something for the wife. I shook my head and left before he could empty my pockets with his smooth sales talk.

I stood on the pavement with an hour to kill and cast an eye along the length of the gaudy amusement arcades. A gruff man, exhibiting all the enthusiasm of someone forced to hand feed piranhas, urged people to try their luck at bingo. Four seats were occupied by elderly folk who tried hard not to let the excitement go to their weakened hearts. The array of exotic prizes included novelty lampshades that would melt on contact with a hot bulb and jigsaw puzzles of Charles and Di.

Hypnotised by the flashing lights I stepped inside in an attempt to rediscover my youth. I went in search of a Space Invader only to discover they'd all been shipped back across the galaxy to be replaced by 'mortal combat' games peopled with ferocious fighting figures leaping around kicking the hell out of each other.

I dug deep, found some change and watched a list of names appear on the screen. I had to be important to have so many people after me. I pressed a button and a sexy woman appeared - things were looking up. But before I could react she was kicking, punching, gouging and throwing me around like a bag of crisps.

I jerked a lever and my character's fist caught her on the chin.

She didn't even blink. She just laughed and threw me into a pile of crates. I tried everything. Sweat was running from my brow, but I was out of my league and she moved in for the kill. All I could do was take it like a man. I reached down and pulled the plug.

It was one-forty. I climbed yet another steep cobbled path, past junk shops and pubs with nautical names, and eventually came to the town centre precinct. The place had certainly taken a turn for the worse. The tiny brick slabs underfoot were mostly cracked and stained by pigeon droppings. Large, overgrown flowerpots with plants trailing in every direction were littered with sweet wrappers and fag ends. Next to them youngsters huddled in groups, happy in the pretence that hanging out was cool.

What remained of the Victorian architecture had been pushed high into the sky by stained glass windows that displayed the passing of time. Slogans ranged from 'Under New Management', to 'End of Season Sale', or 'Closing Down Bargains' to 'somebody please clean me' written in the grime by some smart Alec. The place was falling apart and nobody gave a damn.

I imagined a lone tourist stepping from the train in the not too distant future, walking into the empty precinct to stand and watch the tumbleweed drift past a discarded newspaper, its headline crying, 'East Coast Resort Closes Through Lack of Interest'.

The street was lined with an array of buskers all displaying their talents. A man on an electric piano keyed in a drum beat and sang a variety of Irish tunes that had people whistling along and tapping their feet as they filled his floppy hat. Further along a saxophone player struggled to hit the right notes, and I guessed he would never make enough for his bus fare home. A juggler momentarily impressed the 'three men and a dog' audience with flying axes and flaming batons. But the scorched eyebrows and scarred limbs told me he had some way to go yet.

A small crowd had gathered around a young lad playing a guitar. He was accompanied by April, and if the crowd was in luck April would sing. She had a voice to die for. Although the make-up thin tattered dress didn't suit her. Not surprising perhaps, given that April was a three-year-old dog. It looked in need of food. Its owner looked in need of a bath, but they were better than anything they charged for in the theatres. I dropped some coins onto a rug and headed down the road.

Helen Fitzsimmons' shop was halfway along a narrow side street. It looked the same as the first shop. The girl behind the counter didn't notice me enter. She was too busy staring out of the window, watching the world pass by. I could have stripped the shop bare and she wouldn't have blinked.

"Excuse me," I said, "I'm looking for Helen Fitzsimmons."

"She's out back."

I looked at her with what I hoped was encouragement and with a heavy sigh she dragged her equally heavy shoes 'out back' and bellowed for Mrs Fitzsimmons.

A minute later Helen Fitzsimmons emerged with a smile, looking as elegant as the first time we'd met. She was dressed in a suit, a tight-fitting jacket and trousers that hugged her figure and caressed my hormones. She was pleased to see me and beckoned me with a painted nail.

"Mr Mahoney. How nice to see you again," she beamed.

"Thanks," I replied, my ego swelling. "Nice place," I lied.

"Oh, you like it?"

"No, not really," I confessed.

She didn't appear put out. "I do like your honesty, Mr Mahoney."

Little did she know.

"So . . . do you have any news?"

"Maybe." My eyes surveyed the shop. "Is it all right to talk here?"

"Oh yes," she replied, taking out a cigarette. "The more open and up front one is the less suspicious one appears, don't you think?"

I nodded and forced an uncomfortable smile. "To be honest, not a lot has happened, not until last night anyway."

"Oh, tell me more!"

"Well, Colin took a drive down to the pier and met a someone, a woman."

A glint appeared in her eyes, bright enough to stop her lighting the cigarette.

"Who?"

"I don't know. It was dark and wet and she was covered up. I took some photos, but I doubt they'll show anything."

"What did they do?"

"Talked, for a couple of minutes. Then she drove off and he went home."

"Mmmm," she mused thoughtfully.

The cigarette was waiting in her hand and it stayed there as a man entered the shop and walked over to join us. He reached out towards Helen and they pecked each other on the cheek.

"Frank, I'd like you to meet Richard Mahoney. He's a Private Investigator," she added theatrically.

"Is that right?"

No, I thought, but it'll do for now.

We shook hands. Frank was short, with thick black hair gelled back like some Italian hoodlum. His eyes were large and round, the kind of eyes that could follow you long after their owner was out of sight. His clothes were expensive, but the tie was loud and should have come with a volume control.

"Frank works for the council. He has a very important job, don't you, Frank."

Frank looked back at her and nodded. "I hope you're not in any kind of trouble, Helen." His voice was soft but sincere, it even suggested concern.

"Oh don't be silly, Frank. Mr Mahoney was just looking round the shop and we got talking. Isn't that right, Mr Mahoney?"

"Yeah," I lied, studying the pin on his lapel. It was an image of the castle. Perhaps Frank had been conned by the young salesman in the other shop.

Helen Fitzsimmons grabbed me by the arm and quickly led me towards the door. "You must forgive me. Frank's a charming man but I would rather the less people knew about this little affair, the better."

"Sure."

We stopped at the door.

"So," she hissed mysteriously, "what do you make of this woman?"

I shrugged and wondered what I should make of someone I'd only seen from a distance and in the dark.

"Perhaps you can find out who she is. It could be that she's putting ideas into Colin's head."

"What sort of ideas?"

"I'm not sure. That's what I'd like you to find out."

I glanced across at Frank. He was holding one of the plastic castles but all the while his eyes kept looking back towards Helen.

"Is there a problem, Mr Mahoney?"

"Only that this might be a complete waste of my time and your money."

The glint in her eye had returned. She reached out and touched my arm. "Don't you worry yourself about that, Mr Mahoney. If you are wasting your time and my money, then obviously I was wrong and Colin isn't up to anything after all!"

"And if he is?"

"Then I'm sure I can trust you to do whatever is necessary . . ."

8

That evening I bought a local paper, more out of curiosity than anything else. I wanted to know what had happened in Scarborough that warranted hacking down a rainforest. There were the usual ads for second-hand goods, cars, furniture, and people desperate not to spend another night alone. Numerous columns were accompanied by photographs of journalists, something that always puzzled me. Was it vanity? Or did they really believe their mugshots added credibility to their articles?

Almost everything about the paper either revelled in the past, or looked ominously towards a future that appeared riddled with little or no expectation. The Editor appeared intent on pressuring the council into stemming a drastic decline in the tourist industry. He voiced concern over the shelving of plans for an extravagant indoor 'waterworld' and multiplex cinema that had already met with strong local opposition. Pages celebrated the town during the war, the town before the war, and the good old days.

I peered closely at the pictures of a packed and busy foreshore, and of a harbour with a fishing fleet the size of an armada. Where it had all gone wrong?

A short report by Eddie Hartless drew my attention to Ron Higgens, a pensioner whose wife had died when The Gables hotel had collapsed into the sea. I recalled seeing it on the News at Ten. There had been a flood of jokes doing the rounds at the time; how the Scarborough hotel business was on the rocks, and that the ten-minute walk to the beach was now only two. But sixty-eight-year-old Ron hadn't seen the funny side. He and his wife had spent every summer for the last forty-three years at The Gables. It was their home from home. Hartless was doing his best to stir up interest, but it was old news and not in the spirit of the 'good old days' feel to the paper. Which probably explained why the story was buried at the foot of the page.

I couldn't help thinking about poor old Ron, shuffling round his two-up, two-down in Macclesfield in a pair of worn slippers, stoking the fire, polishing a medal and dusting a photo of himself and his wife, not really understanding why she wasn't there any more.

I poured myself another coffee as the fading light outside slipped into darkness. It was like the car had been swept into a tunnel. I glanced up at the sky and the dirty grey cloud moving slowly overhead. It was times like this you knew you were going to get wet.

Fitzsimmons stepped onto the street and lit a cigarette. I took a shot of him flicking the spent match across the pavement. He looked up at the sky and scowled as if the gathering clouds had been sent to ruin his plans. He locked up, but didn't pop next door to buy a paper. Instead he made his way over to his car.

I started the engine and followed . . . for about a hundred yards, bumping and grinding to a shuddering halt in the middle of the road. I thumped the dash and the petrol gauge needle plummeted like a stone. The tank was empty.

That never happened to Marlowe.

I had to walk half the length of the god-forsaken place to get petrol. Which wasn't nearly as bad as the walk back with two heavy cans of four star.

I pulled up outside number twenty-two half an hour later, hot and tired. Fortunately it didn't appear I'd missed anything. Fitzsimmons' car was parked outside and there was a light on in a downstairs window. I got set for another long night; him all snug and warm and me outside in the cold with no coffee and the smell of petrol everywhere.

It was five past nine. I had started to pull at a reel of tape that had wrapped itself around the guts of the cassette player when I looked up and noticed a figure outside the house. A woman, with all the appearance of someone who'd stepped straight from the pages of a mystery novel. She looked like the woman on the pier. She was wearing the same long coat and heels. With the hood pulled down low she looked and moved like a shadow.

She stepped to the door and rang the bell. Fitzsimmons pulled it open as if he'd been waiting. I managed to get a shot of them standing together in the doorway and another of the door slamming shut.

I clicked on the radio and listened to the news. It was the same news every night, only the names changed. And for thirty-three minutes I sat and waited. I wiped the windows clear of condensation and read the paper, again. Then I wiped the windows again and unravelled a bit more tape. I even completed a crossword puzzle - well almost, three across had me stumped. Then I wiped the window a third time and thought 'why the hell am I waiting?'

If Colin Fitzsimmons and the mystery woman were up to something they were hardly going to put an ad in the local rag or pull back the curtains and turn on the light.

I had to get closer.

I locked the car and headed across the road just as it began to spit. I searched the sky overhead for Divine intervention, but all I got was a faceful of rain. The sudden downpour emptied the street, except for a madman walking his dog and whistling.

I stood at the foot of the concrete steps and looked up at the window. The lights had gone out. I didn't have a plan. I was making things up as I went along. I determined to knock and introduce myself as the electrician, plumber, gasman, anyone, as long as it got me inside.

But I didn't have to do or say anything. The door was already swinging open.

Helen Fitzsimmons wanted dirt, and this was an open invitation . . .

The door clicked to a close behind me, shutting out the rain and leaving me alone in the quiet darkness. Total darkness. It was so dark I couldn't see my hand in front of my face.

A sudden flash of lightning scared me half to death as it lit the hallway, showing the door a few yards to my left. I waited for the heavy rumble of thunder before moving forward, hand outstretched, feeling my way along the wall. It was cold and bare. My mind conjured up images of spiders scurrying towards my fingers, of the floor opening and dropping me into a shark infested pool à la Bond.

I didn't want to take another step. I had always sworn that anyone daft enough to wander around in total darkness, like they do in horror movies, deserved what they got. And yet there I was, just as deserving!

The cold air made me shiver and the rain on my face turned to sweat as my eyes strained into the darkness. I reached the door and pushed it open. In the background my over-active imagination heard the eerie music building to a crescendo. All was about to be revealed, and I didn't like it.

The searching beam from the streetlamp outside slipped in through a chink in the curtains and slid across the floor. Somebody was lying there. Two people were lying there. Very quiet . . . and very still.

Another streak of lightning sliced through the dimness and the thunder crashed overhead.

Neither body moved.

I stepped into the room. "Fitzsimmons," I hissed.

There was no reply.

I'd just stepped into more trouble than I could handle.

9

The man's scuffed shoes almost touched the floor. His head was up in the darkness, inches from the two by four that held up the roof. He was hanging by a length of black electrical wire. His toes were pointed down as if he were standing on tiptoes. I touched him, just enough to discover he was cold and there was no point in cutting him down. He'd made sure of death. It was obvious he'd stood by the sink in the kitchen to knot the short length of rubber tube around his arm prior to clenching his fist to make the vein stand out and shoot the morphine sulphate into his bloodstream. Since all three of the discarded vials littering the drainer were empty, it was a fair assumption that at least one had been full.

That's how Marlowe had found Mitchell in *'Playback'*. Marlowe was cool. Detailed. Precise. Nothing missed. He had pieced together the series of events with elementary precision and without emotion. It was just another body, another piece of the jigsaw that had a place in the puzzle and somehow, some way, he would put it all together.

Unfortunately I wasn't so cool, or detailed. My stomach heaved and my head spun. I clapped a hand across my mouth and rushed into the bathroom. Only it wasn't the bathroom, it was a bedroom. I just made it across the hallway and knelt staring at the marble basin, trying not to recognise everything I'd eaten over the last couple of days. My stomach was twisted into a knot and I heaved and sucked on fresh air until I swore my guts would explode.

Ten minutes later it was over. Sweat poured from my brow. I felt weak and dizzy. The room revolved, even taking cautious steps. I squeezed my mouth under the tap and sipped at the water. I didn't feel good, but I felt a whole lot better.

I wanted to take a look around the apartment but the lights didn't work. There was no power anywhere. I stumbled around in the faint stream of light filtering in from the street and the momentary flashes of lightning.

The place was 'average', and that was being kind. There were two upstairs rooms; a bathroom with plain purple tiles, a toothbrush, toothpaste and a shower; and a bedroom with a large movie poster from Taxi Driver on the wall above a king-size bed. The wardrobe was full of black denim jeans and an array of black and purple shirts. There were no designer labels.

In the kitchen the fridge was practically starved of contents save for a bottle of milk, and two cans of John Smith's. A mouldy, half-eaten loaf lay on a breadboard on the worktop which was littered with crumbs and wrappers.

Fitzsimmons certainly lived a simple life.

I went back into the corridor and waited a moment before stepping back into the lounge. I didn't want to chance shocking myself all over again. I took a deep breath and moved forward.

The room smelt of smoke and dust covers, just like his shop. There were stacks of records (the old-fashioned vinyl type, not the shining silver CD variety) lining the walls. I noticed they weren't filed alphabetically. Perhaps he'd simply shoved them onto the shelves as he'd acquired them. Or perhaps he was just too damn lazy to get around to cataloguing them properly . . . somehow it seemed important.

Dust lay thick and undisturbed on the windowsill, giving the place that 'male' touch. A photo above the fireplace was a close-up of Fitzsimmons. He was holding a beer and smiling like he'd just invited the world to a party. The TV stood silent in the furthest corner, on top of a video recorder and a box of tapes. Films were stacked against the wall including Taxi Driver, The Godfather collection, Star Wars, Jaws, and Raiders of the Lost Ark. It didn't say a lot about the man, but it said a hell of a lot about his tastes.

The bodies lay sprawled, unmoving, across the floor, congealing blood pooled on the lino. A gun was nearby, pointing in the direction of Fitzsimmons. I touched the barrel, it was still hot. Each looked to have a small circular hole in their head, and I felt the bile rising again.

The girl was still wearing her coat and somehow that seemed important too . . . if only I could figure out why. Fitzsimmons was wearing the same jumper he'd had on the day before. It looked like Fitzsimmons had shot the girl before turning the gun on himself. But why? What was I seeing that was trying to give me the answer?

Headlines flashed across my mind, 'Two Die in Lovers' Suicide Pact'. The local plod would go through the futile motions of appealing for witnesses. The elderly would write a slew of letters commenting on how awful things were these days and how it wasn't safe to sleep in your own bed at night. Cameras and reporters would converge on the sleepy little town and the police would ask a lot of useless questions. Two weeks later the case would be filed away under unsolved and everything would return to normal.

I crouched over the girl. She was young, and pretty. She belonged in a nightclub dancing with friends, or planning a holiday in the sun, not lying lifeless here. Her right arm stretched out across the floor like a goalkeeper's despairing dive. I didn't want to touch anything, not until the police arrived. But there was something that intrigued me. Something that caused me to take a closer look.

On the lino, next to her little black shoulder bag, were a couple of strips of negatives.

I knelt there thinking they could be of anything. Holiday snaps, a family photo, a girls' night out. I picked them up between finger and thumb and held them up to the faint light from the window. But it wasn't enough to make anything out.

I lay them in the palm of my hand and considered the possibilities. I'd wandered uninvited into a room to find two bodies. There was no one else in sight.

Marlowe, I knew, would already have the prints in his pocket. He had a job to do. He was being paid a lot of money and they might be the kind of dirt his client was looking for. But Marlowe was a detective. I was a writer. The negatives might keep him out of trouble, but they would get me into a whole lot more. He was a professional. I was an amateur, a novice. He was logical. I was creative.

But none of that stopped me wondering . . .

10

There was no phone in the flat. I had to call the police from a call-box across the street. I told them what I'd seen, but not what I'd found. It took them a while to cotton on to the fact I wasn't joking. I was told to wait, not to touch anything and that somebody would be along in a few minutes.

I didn't mind waiting, the rain had stopped and the cool air was far more refreshing than the smell of the two bodies. I stood wondering what to tell the police. I had found two bodies in a house.

'How?'

'Because I was following them.'

'Why?'

'Because I'm a Private Investigator.'

It didn't sound at all convincing.

But was I meant to tell the truth, or could I lie, because surely all that mattered was that I'd found them. Two people who'd been killed. It needed investigating, they might have wasted there for ages if I hadn't stuck my nose in.

Even then it didn't sound convincing.

~

The police arrived twenty minutes later. And it was a bit of a let down. There were no screaming sirens, blue flashing lights, screeching tyres, or armed officers in flak jackets crouching down behind parked cars pointing rifles at anything that moved. Instead a single patrol car ambled up and I watched in amazement as the driver tried three times to squeeze into a parking space. Eventually he gave up and double parked.

Two men got out and came towards me. The younger man, in a long raincoat, led an older man who looked like he had the weight of the world on his shoulders.

The young one pointed at me. "Are you the guy who rang us?"

"Yeah."

"They didn't give us your name."

"It's er, Mahoney, Richard Mahoney."

"Right. I'm Sergeant O'Neal and this is Inspector Walker."

We nodded at one another like Indians around a camp fire. Then O'Neal pointed to number twenty-two. "In there?"

I nodded again. And, without waiting for the troops to arrive, we set off up the steps to the house. I could have been over-reacting, but I couldn't help noticing that neither carried a gun. It all seemed very 'British'. There we were making our way towards a house in which two people had been shot and all we had to protect ourselves was strength of character and a torch.

We slipped into the hallway and I motioned to the door on our left. O'Neal pushed it open and stepped inside. Walker followed. I brought up the rear and therefore was the last to realise that the light was on and that both policemen were staring at me.

I glanced down at the floor. It was clean. Empty. Untouched. There were no bodies. There was no blood. Nothing.

It was the right house. And it was the right room . . . "They were here! Right there, on the floor . . . the pair of them!"

"Are you sure they were dead, Mr Mahoney?"

I glared at O'Neal. What a daft question! "There was a gun, they'd been shot, there was blood everywhere!"

He stared at me and bit his lip. There was a look of suspicion in his eyes.

"Have you ever seen a dead body before, Mr Mahoney?"

O'Neal was playing me for a fool and I didn't blame him. Ever since I'd arrived in town I'd been holding all the Jokers.

"What the Sergeant is getting at," Walker said quietly, "is that maybe somebody was playing a trick on you. It happens."

A trick! But what about the bodies? They were stone cold. They were dead!

O'Neal wandered across to the light switch and tapped it with his pencil. "You said the power was off, right?"

"Right!"

He flicked the switch on and off. The lights worked perfectly. It wasn't looking good.

"But they weren't working!" I said.

"So, I assume the place would have been quite dark?"

If stating the obvious had been a crime, O'Neal would have been hung, drawn and quartered by now.

"Yeah!"

"Therefore it would be very difficult to know exactly what it was you were looking at. If you know what I mean?"

"I know what I saw, Sergeant!" I scowled.

But O'Neal wasn't convinced. He made a lot of noise pulling up a chair and getting out his notebook. He wanted to make sure I saw the look in his eye, the one a teacher gives a pupil who's been caught smoking behind the bike shed.

I tried to not appear bothered, but I was. I was sure Marlowe wouldn't have liked O'Neal. He was a rookie cop, straight out of university. Sure, he wore the stripes, but he had none of the scars. His tie was straight, his collar pressed, his shoes shiny and neatly laced and he filled his notebook with lead like Cagney filled his enemies.

"Tell me," he said, licking the tip of his pencil, "these people, were they friends of yours ?"

"No . . ." I saw the look that passed between them. ". . . I was following them."

"Why?"

"Why?"

"Yes. Why were you following them?"

This shouldn't have been happening. I'd reported two dead bodies. I'd done the right thing - a good deed. Now it felt like the world was closing in on me.

"Because . . . because I'm a Private Investigator."

"That's funny . . ." O'Neal said without smiling. "I've never heard of you."

"Are you in the habit of looking up PIs?" I snapped.

O'Neal crossed his legs and stared silently at me.

"I work with Ronnie Elliott," I said. "I'm his partner."

Walker circled the room in front of me. Up to now he hadn't said much.

"Ronnie?" he said casually. "You work with Ronnie Elliott?"

I nodded. "You've heard of him then?"

"Of course I have. . . he's a slob."

It may have sounded a harsh, but I couldn't really argue otherwise.

Walker crossed the room with large, heavy feet and just about made it to a chair. He pulled out a cigar, the kind you needed a blowtorch to light, and ran it slowly under his nose while O'Neal tapped his pencil.

"So you say you were following them?"

"No. Just the man. I only saw the girl for the first time tonight."

Walker leaned forward and lit the cigar. The flare of the match lit his features. His face was round and worn. He had a jaw the size of a shovel and twice as smooth.

"I take it somebody asked you to follow him?" he asked.

I nodded.

"Would you mind telling us who exactly?"

It was O'Neal who asked the question, but I was looking at Walker. I tried to recall a film starring Robert Mitchum. A girl he'd been following had jumped from a window. The police wanted to know why but he confidently referred to client confidentiality. Not so confidently, I tried the same thing.

"Do I have to?"

Walker rolled his eyes heavenward while O'Neal folded away his notebook.

"Is that it?"

Walker sounded surprised. "Is that it? What do you mean, is that it?"

"Is that all you're going to do?"

"And what exactly would you like me to do, Mahoney? Examine the bodies perhaps? Oh, but there aren't any! Talk to your client perhaps? Oh, but . . ."

"You don't believe me!"

The Inspector pressed a thumb and forefinger deep into his eyes and let out a heavy sigh. "How long were you gone after you found the bodies?"

"I don't know. About twenty minutes I guess."

"And did you see anyone else enter or leave?"

I didn't answer.

"Did you see . . ."

"No!"

Walker was happier now. He'd dug a hole for me to fall into and was content to leave me floundering about in it without so much as a ladder.

"Look at it from my point of view, Mahoney. Half an hour ago, I was drinking coffee and throwing darts at the door. Just another night at the station. I was happy. Everybody was happy. Then we get a call from someone claiming to have found a couple of stiffs . . . isn't that how you PI-types refer to them?" I winced. "When I finally get here, these so-called bodies have up and left without so much as a by-your-leave, kiss my arse or anything. And now I am unhappy . . . very unhappy!"

"I didn't realise I was meant to be entertaining you!"

"You're not!"

"So you're saying I made all this up?"

"I haven't said any such thing." Walker's stare was cold and long.

I slowly circled the room. I was running out of options.

"Helen Fitzsimmons," I mumbled reluctantly.

"Who?"

"Helen Fitzsimmons . . . my client."

"*The* Helen Fitzsimmons?" O'Neal asked, flashing a triumphant smile at Walker.

"Yeah. She asked me to follow her ex. He lives here."

"Is that who you allegedly found lying on the floor?"

"No . . . that's who I 'actually' found lying on the floor!"

Walker took a deep breath before nodding at O'Neal. The Sergeant pulled out a mobile phone and asked for the operator. Walker dipped his hands deep into his baggy trousers and sat down. He was saying something about how this wasn't going to do any good because, even if Helen Fitzsimmons did confirm my story, there were still no bodies and nothing to go on . . . but I was watching O'Neal, trying to read his lips. He looked bothered. He put his hand over the receiver and glanced across at me.

"Mrs Fitzsimmons says she remembers talking to you, but that all you discussed was legal advice. She says she never asked you to follow . . ."

I flew at him and snatched the phone. It was the most positive thing I'd done all day.

"That's ridiculous," I yelled. "Hello!"

But the phone had gone dead.

"Hello! Hello!"

O'Neal prised the phone out of my grasp and wiped the mouthpiece with a handkerchief. It might have bothered me, had not everything else started to.

Walker stood up and shrugged apologetically. "If anyone reports anyone missing we'll get back to you. In the meantime, I've had a long night and I'm desperate for some coffee."

O'Neal closed the door behind them.

Everything was as it had been earlier, with the thunder beating a tattoo on the clouds outside and the moon shining through the window. Only the bodies were missing.

~

The walk back to the car seemed to take forever. My feet were heavy, my eyes tired and I sensed that every eye in the street was watching me. Through slits in the curtains little people with little lives and even less to live for probably wondered who this idiot was wasting valauable police time.

I was so out of my depth I needed water wings. I'd come here looking for inspiration and instead had run headlong into a PI with all the class of a drunk violinist on a high wire. I'd lied about being a PI, not only to Helen Fitzsimmons, but to the police as well. If I'd been looking for trouble I wasn't having any difficulty finding it. By the time I reached the car I'd come to the conclusion that things couldn't get any worse.

I was wrong.

The car had had both its nearside tyres slashed. Things had just got a whole lot worse.

~

I dreamed I was walking along the pier. I was alone. The pier was four feet wide and the timber was rotten. It stretched ahead of me, far out into the darkness. Waves the size of houses crashed down on either side of me, threatening to sweep me away at any moment.

I was heading out along the pier towards Helen Fitzsimmons. She was smiling, assuring me everything was all right. There was someone behind me. I couldn't see who it was, but I knew it was Walker. I could smell the cigar. He was calling my name, warning me not to go any further. He was calling me by my real name. 'Tony,' he called, 'don't go any further. Come back, Tony. Come back now!' But I couldn't take my eyes off Helen Fitzsimmons.

She was wearing a long, tight dress. It hugged her figure like a second skin. She raised her hand and beckoned me on, her fingers straining against the weight of diamond rings. The jewels sparkled in the darkness, almost blinding me.

I walked forever, but she got no nearer. And all the while Walker's voice grew ever louder.

There was no breeze. No salt on the air. Just the crash of the mountainous waves and the smell of that vile cigar. I took another step and Walker yelled out, 'No!'

A piece of timber gave way beneath me and my foot slipped through the gap. The pain was incredible. The pier wrapped itself around my calf. No matter how much I struggled my leg remained trapped. I pulled so hard it felt like the bones would snap.

Helen Fitzsimmons stood over me, smiling . . . I screamed and woke, dripping with perspiration.

Through the windscreen dawn broke over a harsh silhouette of hotels and guest houses and slowly everything came together. Fitzsimmons, bodies, police, no bodies, angry police, embarrassment, flat tyres, sleep in the car, nightmare . . .

This wasn't how things had been meant to be.

I stepped from the car haggard and creased like someone who'd spent the night in a thimble. It took me a good half hour to straighten my limbs and another to change the second tyre after walking a mile to a seedy back-street garage.

All the while I kept half an eye on Fitzsimmons' house, wondering if, or when he might show up. But he didn't. Nothing happened.

Eventually I decided to leave and try his shop.

It was closed. The old woman in the newsagent's next door told me it wasn't unusual for Fitzsimmons to just up and leave 'on business' for a week or more without a word to anyone.

I was running out of ideas and with them any inspiration.

I called into the office but Ronnie wasn't there; everything was as it had been when I'd left it, a mess. I sat on the desk and watched the world creep by the window. Something had to give, but I didn't know what and I didn't know when.

There was a knock and I turned to see two suits standing in the doorway; a short stocky suit and a gorilla dressed in pinstripes.

Short Suit inched towards me. Close enough for me to see that his eyes were set so far back into his skull that it was like looking into a pair of binoculars. A jagged scar ran down from the bottom of his left ear to the curl of his lip like someone had enjoyed feeding him bottles.

"Richard Mahoney?"

My reputation was spreading.

"Yeah. Take a seat."

"We're not stopping."

"What can I do for you?"

"Actually," he said, striking a match on the heel of his shoe. It was a neat trick but hardly worth the smirk pasted across his face, ". . . you don't mind if I smoke, do you?"

"Not if you're not stopping."

"Actually," he resumed, "it's what we can do for you."

I was intrigued. I sat in my chair and wondered what on earth the ill-matched pair could possibly do for me, short of moving my furniture.

"The word is that you're working for Helen Fitzsimmons."

"The word?"

He nodded.

"Whose word?" I asked.

"That doesn't matter."

"It might to me!"

"No! What matters to you is that you no longer work for Mrs Fitzsimmons."

I glanced at Short Suit and then at his buddy, the gorilla. He hadn't moved an inch and that was probably just as well. Judging by the size of him he could probably do some real damage if he wanted to.

"I've seen the colour of her money," I quipped. "So I know she's not going to sell me short, so this must be a threat."

Short Suit shrugged and ran the tip of a finger down the length of his scar.

"I prefer to think of it as a piece of advice, friendly advice, you understand."

"Oh, I understand. It's the kind of advice that might have me swimming in the sea with a pair of concrete waders if I ignore it!"

Short Suit glanced at the gorilla. "I hadn't thought of that."

Me and my big mouth.

I got to my feet. The gorilla took a couple of paces towards me and he wasn't looking to shake my hand. I sat back down. The gorilla backed off.

"And what do I tell my client, assuming the word is right of course?"

"You can tell her what you like."

"But I need to make a living. I've got bills to pay just like everyone else."

Short Suit wandered over to the window and looked out. "Have you lived here long, Mr Mahoney?"

"About three days."

"Well, let me tell you, this used to be a nice town. It was full of nice people who looked out for one another. Anybody put a brick through a window, they'd wake up in hospital with a broken nose. That's how it is . . . how it was," he corrected himself. "Now nobody cares, people don't look you in the eye and call you by your first name. Nobody offers anybody a lift and that isn't good, Mahoney, that's never been any good."

"And what's all that got to do with me?"

Short Suit pointed his cigarette at me. "You look like somebody who cares."

"Maybe you just caught me on a good day . . ."

"I don't think so. I think you care, I think you care a lot, and that's what these people need, somebody who cares, somebody who's willing to put things right."

"Maybe Mrs Fitzsimmons wants things put right?"

"Maybe she does. Maybe she doesn't. But she's got brass, and she can take care of herself. You need to take care of the little guys!"

He was resting the palms of his hands on the desk and looking down at me.

"So you want me to go round breaking noses every time somebody puts a brick through a window?"

"Actually," he snarled, leaning in real close, "I'm telling you not to go looking for trouble. Start looking after the nice people and don't go worrying about the rich."

I felt for all the world as though he'd finish the sentence with 'you know what I'm saying?' It would have rounded the whole thing off perfectly. But he didn't. Instead the two of them turned and left. They even closed the door behind them.

They were gone but the stale smell of cigarette smoke still lingered and it made me uncomfortable.

There were any number of ways a PI could get himself killed, but second-hand smoke wasn't the one for me. It just didn't have that 'hero's death' kind of feel about it.

I stepped outside and decided on another trip to Spillanes. The stage was dark and empty, there was no blues, no Ronnie, nothing.

This time I ordered a coffee. I needed time to think and I needed a clear head to do my thinking in. I skimmed through a local paper that someone had left lying around, expecting to see something, a line or two, about the police being called out in the early hours of the morning to a disturbance at number twenty-two. But there was nothing.

A young couple had returned from a funeral to find their house ransacked, and somebody by the name of Hilda had celebrated her hundredth birthday with a telegram from the Queen.

I got the distinct impression nobody cared about Colin Fitzsimmons, or the girl.

I was about to leave when Mandy stepped up to me, smiling. She was wearing legs for earrings and just enough blouse to keep my imagination from wandering. She sat down next to me and purred, "Hello, Mr Private Investigator."

"Hi," I replied. "I wasn't expecting to see you."

She appeared hurt. "Oh, and there's me thinking that's why you were here."

Women just didn't say things like that to me.

"Would you like a drink?" I asked.

She nodded and ordered a rum and coke with plenty of ice. I paid the barmaid and glanced back at Mandy. I couldn't help thinking how she had the air of someone who knew what she wanted and knew how to get it. She placed her drink on the table and swept a loose strand of hair out of her eyes.

"So, did you find Ronnie?"

I shook my head.

"And what about your client?"

"I got brave."

"You saw her?" she asked, inching her legs closer to mine. Again I nodded. "What happened?"

"I told her I was Ronnie's partner."

"And she bought it?"

"Hook, line and sinker."

A hand reached out under the table and pressed my knee. The rest of my body raged with jealousy.

"What did she want you to do?"

"Follow someone."

"Who?"

"Somebody she used to know. Her ex-husband."

"This is quite exciting. Who is she? If you don't mind me asking?"

I should have minded, but talking to her was a whole lot better than talking to myself.

"Helen Fitzsimmons," I said, quietly.

Her eyebrows almost disappeared over the top of her head. "*The* Helen Fitzsimmons?"

"Why does everybody keep doing that?" I asked.

"Doing what?"

"Saying her name that way."

"Because she's a big name around here, big for this dump anyway." She took another sip and looked at me. "So what happened?"

I don't know why, but I told her everything. I mean, I didn't know her from Adam, but somehow it felt good to have someone who would listen and take an interest, someone who didn't look at me like Walker and O'Neal had, like I'd just escaped from an asylum.

"So what happens now?"

"I don't know," I confessed.

"What do you mean you don't know?"

"I mean I don't know what Mrs Fitzsimmons wants me to do. After all, she's the one paying the bills."

"She's also the one lying to you!"

"Yeah, I forgot about that." I looked down into my cup. "I wish Ronnie would turn up."

She took my hand. "Look, forget about Ronnie, you've got to look after yourself. You've got to find out what's going on. You're sure those two people were dead, aren't you?"

I nodded.

"Then prove it."

"How? I can't even prove I'm a PI!"

"If you prove one, you'll prove the other . . ."

I listened long and I listened hard and, try as I might, I couldn't find fault with anything she told me. Mandy not only had great legs but a brain to match and I couldn't resist either.

~

I drove along the foreshore. The early evening clouds were kicking up a storm. A westerly wind sliced through the sea leaving a trail of white foaming manes in its wake. But the sea roared on, rising high above the harbour wall, before crashing down onto the empty road and then rushing back out beyond the dark horizon.

Behind me rose the clamour of the amusement arcades and I thought of the pinball, propelled from its bed and sent spinning around a maze of flashing lights and ringing bells. Trapped and bounced from inspiration to criticism, knowing its only purpose was to try and accumulate as many points as possible before disappearing down that big black hole. Helen Fitzsimmons had taken me for a ride.

Asking me to follow her ex-husband simply because he might be up to something was one thing. Finding Colin and the girl dead was another. But for her to deny knowing me to the police wasn't a good sign.

I called in at her foreshore shop, but she wasn't there. The young man behind the counter told me she'd gone away for the day. How convenient, I thought.

Outside, buffeted by the biting wind, I wondered what to do next. Maybe caring was my weakness. I wasn't a detective and I was deluding myself to think I ever could be. Being a detective took years of practice and dedication. People didn't just step out of their normal lives and suddenly change the world for the better.

I was irritable. It may have been the realisation that I might never fulfil my dreams.

I needed a break. I needed inspiration. I needed a beer . . .

~

I drove to the library. I was late. The session had already started. Sophie was reading a passage from her novel. Everybody looked towards the door as I stepped inside. I'm not sure if they were annoyed or slightly relieved at my intrusion. Ms Simms smiled and pointed to a chair. I sat down and Sophie went back to her reading.

From what I could gather she was writing about a girl travelling from one end of the country to the other. It was a voyage of discovery. It was deep, very deep, so deep that I was soon up to my neck in words and phrases I'd never even heard. I had no idea what she was talking about. Apparently Sophie was an artist, her work spoke volumes, and that was just as well, bearing in mind that nobody else could get a word in edgeways

I decided to stare at Trish. She was wearing blue jeans and black ankle boots. She looked good, she looked better than good and although she never glanced in my direction, I could tell she knew I was staring by the way the hint of a smile played around her lips every so often. I wanted to know if she was going to the pub afterwards or if she had somebody to meet, a boyfriend, a fiancé, a husband.

A round of applause woke me from my daydreaming. Sophie was milking the praise of the group with an air that suggested they were only telling her what she already knew.

I listened impatiently to the back-patting until Ms Simms looked across at me and asked if I'd like to tell the group about my novel. My heart bounced across the floor and rolled out of the door.

"But I haven't . . . I haven't actually written anything yet."

"That's all right, maybe you could just outline the story for us and give us an insight into the main characters. I'm sure we'd all be very interested."

I glanced around the room and everybody nodded as if to suggest that they were very interested indeed. I coughed and stuttered, cleared my throat and told them what I had so far. I began with Mahoney waking up in an office to the ringing of the phone and finished with two bodies lying on the floor. And all the time I couldn't help thinking how, in the cold light of day, it all sounded so unconvincing. My story lacked panache. Every word came out like a nail being pulled from a lump of wood. When I finished I glanced quickly up at Ms Simms and then cast my eyes down onto the table in front of me. The silence that followed was heartbreaking. It engulfed my hopes and desires and spat them out across the room in a big ugly heap. I wanted everybody to be frozen in time so I could just get up and leave, never to return.

Eventually Ms Simms asked if anybody had anything to say. Gerald raised a finger and asked what my motive was for the killings. I thought for a moment and then confessed that I wasn't sure and that invited a barrage of stinging criticism. Apparently I had to have a motive, and people were quick to offer me their ideas. I listened intently to suggestions that varied from love triangles to drug dealing, though it transpired that 'revenge' killing was very popular and much in demand.

"And don't forget the children," said Sophie. "There's always children involved . . ."

By the time I'd jotted everything down the room had emptied, all expect for Ms Simms. She took time putting away her notebook and stuck a lock of hair behind her ear for the umpteenth time. I looked down at the scribbled notes and tried to make sense of them. It was as if I'd thrown a pot of paints across a stark white canvas . . .

"Are you all right?" Ms Simms asked as she headed for the door.

"Yes," I lied as people do when they know no one really gives a damn. She smiled goodnight and left.

For a while I sat in silence thinking of home, of walking in the rain and signing on . . . now that was reality. Being here in Scarborough, trying to write a book, pretending to be a detective was just a dream.

Perhaps it was time to go home.

I could hear the beating of the rain before I reached the street door. I stood in the doorway and watched the water slash across the street lights and onto the tarmac below.

"Does it always rain here?" a voice enquired softly.

I turned to see Trish standing in the shadows.

"No, it just seems that way." I closed the door behind me. "Are you waiting for a lift?"

She shook her head. "I was waiting for it to ease up a little."

"Good for you. Personally I'd rather risk drowning."

She raised an eyebrow. It was the closest thing I'd seen to an expression. "It's not that bad."

"Actually, it is. In fact it's worse than bad." I was looking for sympathy, and wasting my time. She lowered her eyebrow and looked out at the rain.

"So what did you expect?"

"I don't know, I've never done this kind of thing before. But a little inspiration wouldn't have gone amiss."

"And where do Private Investigators go when they're seeking inspiration?"

Her question took me by surprise and had me fumbling for an answer. "I . . . I don't know. I mean, I suppose they just follow the clues."

"And hunches?"

"Yeah. And hunches . . ." I conceded.

"And if you were a Private Investigator and somebody came along and said, 'you shouldn't follow that man, you should be following that other man,' what would you say?"

"Well, unless he had a damn good reason I'd probably tell him to mind his own business."

"Exactly."

She was looking at me as if that was that.

The trouble was I wasn't really sure what that was.

"Hang on a minute, are you telling me I shouldn't listen to anyone else?"

"I'm not telling you anything."

"But . . ."

"Why did you come here tonight?"

"I told you, because I'm writing a book and I need help."

"Who says?"

"Me!"

"And how do you know?"

"Because . . . because . . . Hell! I don't know . . ."

Trish looked at me, then at the rain and then back at me again.

"The people who God, or nature, intend to be writers find their own answers, and those who have to ask are impossible to help. They are merely people who 'want to be' writers."

I stood listening to the rain, concentrating on what she'd said. I wasn't sure if she was insulting or encouraging me. "Is that a good thing or a bad thing?"

"That depends on who you are."

"Is that what you think?"

Trish shook her head. "It's not what I think, it's what Chandler wrote."

"Chandler? Raymond Chandler wrote that?"

She nodded.

If Chandler had written it then it had to be true. I couldn't argue with the master.

The rain had eased. Trish stepped out onto the pavement.

"This is your journey," she said. "It's up to you to explore the corridors, to be brave enough to open the doors. Nobody else can."

She was a fount of knowledge, and a very attractive fount at that.

"Did Chandler say that as well?"

Trish shook her head and started down the street. "No, I just did!"

I watched her until she reached the end of the street and turned the corner, never once looking back. It wasn't a good sign. But I didn't feel bad. I couldn't feel bad, the girl of so few words knew Chandler . . . and she had lovely high cheekbones too. What more could I ask for?

I turned up my collar and headed into the night. This was to be the first step of my journey. I didn't merely 'want' to be a writer, I wanted with all my heart and soul to be a writer, a successful writer, so successful that I could buy the obligatory house in the Lake District and go on writing forever . . . it sounded so simple.

All I needed now was some answers.

11

Ronnie Elliot turned up first thing on Monday morning. He'd been swimming . . . in the sea! But Ronnie couldn't swim. He couldn't even doggy paddle, not even if his life depended on it, and it had.

I'd gone to the office. I liked it there. I felt at home. I enjoyed slipping my feet onto the desk and reading the morning paper. I enjoyed staring out of the window watching people hurry by. And I enjoyed the thought of Lauren Bacall stepping into the room with her long legs and 'come to bed' eyes, all ready to teach me how to whistle.

I was standing waiting for the kettle to boil when the phone began to ring.

I let it ring for a while. I didn't want people to think I had nothing better to do than sit around waiting to answer the phone.

It was the police. Inspector Walker wanted to see me. He was at a place called Skelton Mills. I fumbled for a piece of paper and scribbled down the directions. When I asked what it was all about the constable hung up.

I slipped the directions into my coat pocket and looked up to find Helen Fitzsimmons staring back at me. She was framed in the doorway with a 'Mona Lisa smile' etched onto her full red lips. Her expression told me she knew I'd already noted her slim, enticing figure in her clinging red dress. Helen Fitzsimmons had a face and a body to die for and that bothered me. I was too young to die . . .

"And just when I thought my day couldn't get any worse!"

She appeared unmoved. She just smiled and said, "Flattery doesn't come easy to you, does it, Mr Mahoney?"

"Not when someone insists on lying to me."

"Who?"

"You!"

She inched an eyebrow ever so slightly and stepped into the room. She was confident and that was something else about her that bothered me. In fact everything about Helen Fitzsimmons bothered me and that bothered me the most!

"So tell me, when did I lie to you exactly?"

She perched on the edge of the desk and crossed her shapely, nylon encased legs.

"When you told the police we only discussed legal advice."

"Please, Mr Mahoney, I had absolutely no idea what they were calling me about."

She had a point. O'Neal had made no mention of the elusive 'stiffs', or even of the fact that I had been there with him.

"And besides, if I'd wanted the police involved I wouldn't have hired a Private Investigator, would I?"

"Hired?" I said, "Or bought?"

She smiled that same confident smile. "Tell me, Mr Mahoney, are you always this melodramatic?"

"No. But then again, people aren't always trying to take me for a ride."

She looked around the room. It didn't appeal to her. It was dark, dingy and cheap. I had thought about tidying it up, but then it wouldn't have appeared so 'lived in' and a PI's office should always appear lived in - it was one of the golden rules. It was where he spent most of his time. It was his home from home. It gave him a sense of dedication, the feeling that there was no place to go until the job was done, the criminal behind bars and the world was once again a safe place to live.

"Do you have anything to drink?"

When I didn't answer she looked down at me and grimaced, "Please."

I walked to the kettle and flicked the switch. "Tea or coffee?"

"I don't suppose you have something a little stronger?"

I wrenched my eyes away from her legs and rifled the filing cabinet for the remains of the whisky. I handed her the whisky in one of the mugs, it was all there was. She glanced at the mug and then at me.

"I'm sure I've never seen anything so uncouth."

"You should take a look at the bathroom."

She pressed her full red lips to the rim and sipped. She enjoyed it. At least, she enjoyed the effect it had on her. I went back to the kettle and made myself coffee. I'd had enough whisky to last a lifetime.

"So tell me, why did the police call me?"

"They wanted to know why I was following your ex. And right now, so do I."

"I told you . . ."

"Yeah, you figured he might try and pinch some pennies from your old man. Well I don't buy it. Not unless there's proof."

She placed the mug on the desk, stood and reached into her bag for a note. She handed it to me.

I looked at her.

"Go ahead, read it."

I sat down and opened it. There wasn't much to read.

I know what you've done and I'm going to make sure you pay.

"Is somebody blackmailing you?"

"Not me. My father."

"Why didn't you show me this before?"

"Because nobody knows about this, not even my father."

"You open his mail?"

"My father's very ill. He has a weak heart. I'm doing what I can for him and I don't want anybody telling him about this. Do I make myself clear?"

I dropped the note onto the desk. "I thought this was between you and your ex?"

"So did I. But obviously Colin has other ideas and now he wants to involve my father."

I studied her for a moment while she sipped at the whisky. She could obviously handle her drink, but could she handle the truth? And just how close to the truth was she leading me now?

"There was another reason?"

"Yes," she said. "And it has something to do with those ideas running through your mind right now."

"You read minds as well?"

"It doesn't take a lot to know that you'll assume my father's done something to deserve that awful note."

"Well, ten years ago he was a nobody with nothing, now he's the richest man in town. He must have trodden on a few toes, maybe now somebody's looking for a payback."

"It's possible," she murmured softly.

"But you're still convinced it's your ex?"

She nodded.

"Have there been any more notes?"

She shook her head.

"No demands for money?"

"No! Absolutely not."

"Then I've got some good news for you, in a kind of bad way."

Her frown followed me right across the room.

"Colin Fitzsimmons is dead."

She mouthed the word dead as if attempting to say it for the very first time.

"Are . . . are you sure?"

"I've never been so sure of anything in my life. That's why the police rang you the other night. I'd been waiting outside his apartment when that girl turned up again."

"The one you saw him with on the pier?"

"Yeah. You said you wanted some dirt, so I went inside. I found him, and the girl, lying next to one another in a pool of blood."

"And they were . . ." She couldn't bring herself to say it.

I nodded.

"How?"

"They'd been shot."

Helen Fitzsimmons appeared momentarily stunned. The colour had drained from her face.

I poured her another drink and she didn't mind the mug this time.

"What did the police have to say?" she asked eventually, the colour slowly returning to her cheeks.

"Not a lot," I mumbled.

"Why?"

I looked down at the floor and tried to work out what to say next but however hard I tried it still came out a mess. "Because by the time they got there the bodies had disappeared."

I raised my eyes long enough to see the look of shock on her face.

"Disappeared!"

I nodded.

"How?"

"I don't know. I wish I did. It must have happened while I was waiting outside for the police."

"Do you know how ridiculous that sounds?"

"I've heard worse."

"Do you suppose that somebody disposed of them?"

"It's possible."

"But why?"

"I don't know."

"What are you going to do now?"

"I'm not going to do anything!"

"I don't understand. You're surely not going to let two dead bodies disappear just like that and not do anything about it?"

"Why not? The police don't seem to care, so why should I?"

She stood up and straightened her dress. "Perhaps I was wrong about you, after all."

"How's that?"

"I would never have taken you for someone lacking in perseverance."

I looked at Mrs Fitzsimmons. She didn't know the first thing about me, let alone if I was a quitter. She didn't even know she was paying a 'nobody'. But then, she was desperate. Desperate for what exactly, I wasn't sure, but she was desperate all the same.

She took a stroll around the office and looked back at me.

"If Colin is still out there . . ."

"Oh! He's out there all right, but when they fish him out of the water he's going to be leaking like a watering can."

"But you can't be entirely sure, can you!"

"I saw the bodies . . ."

"So you say. But you can't be certain they were dead, can you?"

"I know what I saw!"

"Perhaps, but tell me, the moment you discovered Colin and the girl had disappeared, didn't a tiny seed of doubt slip into your mind?"

We stood face to face, looking into each other's eyes. Anything could have happened. But what did was that she pulled out an envelope and pressed it to my chest. I didn't have to look to know it was full of money. Lots of money.

"I asked you to do something for me, Mr Mahoney, and now I would very much like you to finish what you started."

"What do you want me to do? Dig up every grave and dredge every river in town?"

"Whatever it takes."

"That's asking a lot!"

"I'm paying a lot!"

The door closed. Only the cash and the scent of her perfume remained. Helen Fitzsimmons had a way with words and an even better way with money. She was difficult to ignore and whether I liked it or not I still had a lot of questions desperately needing answers.

~

Skelton Mills was a small cove at farthest end of the town's north bay – that's how posh things used to be around here, a town with two bays. I drove there straight from the office.

I took a right and started down a narrow twisting road until I was brought to a halt by a thin line of orange and white tape. There was a young copper, with an even younger moustache, guarding the tape as if he thought someone might try and steal it. I told him who I was and that I was looking for Walker. He nodded and, lifting the tape, waved me through.

I liked the north bay. It was quiet, still and genteel, in stark contrast to the perpetual noise, motion and stench of the more downbeat south bay. The bright morning sun highlighted a narrow stretch of sand topped by lush grass and picturesque guest houses where plump landladies with rosy cheeks served rashers of bacon like it was going out of fashion. A miniature steam engine sounded its horn and the passengers waved to people dangling high above in the brightly coloured umbrella-style chairlift.

I left the car in the car park and another bobby pointed me towards the beach. A small crowd had gathered on a hill just above the bay and were looking down at the rocks where two men in green overalls were carrying something, or someone, away from the water.

The tide crept in, bringing with it a flock of noisy gulls which dived to feed off the sewage spreading like a slick out from the shore.

I stepped closer and watched the men move onto the pebbled beach and lower the body onto a stretcher. Another police photographer snapped away, taking in every detail, while a stern-faced woman inspected the body.

O'Neal was there, scribbling in his notebook.

I passed close enough to see the body. It was a man in a brown coat.

Beneath the coat was a quilted waistcoat with pearl buttons. He was wearing grey socks and training shoes. It looked like Ronnie Elliott. I edged closer. There was no mistaking that face. I felt strange, surprised. This wasn't meant to be happening. It was like waking from a deep sleep with no idea where I was or what I was doing. My stomach lurched, but I didn't feel sick. Perhaps I was getting used to the sight of corpses . . .

Ronnie didn't look so good. Lying there cold, alone, and covered in seaweed in soaking clothes, he looked bad. I'd only known him for a short time yet I'd convinced myself that he was a waste of space, a slob, the kind of person people crossed the street to avoid. Now I felt shame and guilt. Death can do that to you.

I remembered the day my granddad had died. I loved him. We'd shared so many great times together. Then one night we argued. I was upset about something and I told him to go to hell and we never spoke again. He died the following week and I hadn't had the chance to say I was sorry. For months afterwards all I could think about was granddad going to hell and all because of me . . .

I dragged myself away from the stretcher and stepped down onto the pebbled beech. Walker was there, alone and staring out to sea. He appeared deep in thought. I stood and waited in the silence and a foot of seaweed and brackish water. Eventually he let out a heavy sigh.

"Have you ever been abroad, Mahoney?"

"I went to Wales once."

"No. I mean abroad, like Australia or the Far East."

"No, but I'd like to go to America one day . . ."

"Take my advice," he said, seriously, "don't think about it, do it."

He took out a cigar and studied it closely, his thoughts somewhere else.

"I always wanted to go to Australia," he continued. "I don't know why, I just did. Unfortunately, this is the closest I've got."

He lowered his gaze as a dying wave washed up at our feet and soaked through the pebbles.

"I'm sure there's still time."

He shook his head. "There's always something that gets in the way, always something more important, commitments, responsibilities, you name it, and then one day you wake up and realise it's simply too late."

"Does the sight of a dead body always bring this kind of regret out in you?"

Walker looked at me for a moment. "You'll listen to what I'm saying, Mahoney, if you know what's good for you."

He turned and looked out to sea again, his face tinged with regret. I couldn't make him out. Yesterday he'd hardly noticed me, today he was spilling out his life story and offering free advice. He may have offered more if O'Neal hadn't butted in.

"All they know for certain is that there was a struggle. Elliot has a head wound and there's another wound on his neck, probably made by a knife or a pair of scissors."

"When will they have the post-mortem done?"

"Early evening."

Walker nodded, but didn't look impressed.

"Oh, and how about this? It appears his wrists were bound with something."

Walker looked thoughtfully at O'Neal, but didn't say a word.

I listened to the sound of the waves slapping hard against the rocks and the wind whistling low across the sea. It was a gentle, melodic sound and one I could have gone on listening to had O'Neal not ceased chewing his pencil and asked, "When was the last time you saw Ronnie Elliott, Mr Mahoney?"

"Monday."

"Monday when?"

"Morning. In his office."

"And how did he seem?"

"His usual 'life's a Morrisey record and then you die' self."

"What was he working on?"

"Nothing."

"Nothing?"

"Yeah well, that's the funny thing. He told me what a waste of time it was being here. How nothing ever happens."

There was the sound of doors slamming shut and we turned as one to watch the ambulance pull away.

"So you didn't see or hear him speak to anyone?"

"He took a call from his dad. He told me . . ."

The words trailed off as Walker and O'Neal exchanged knowing glances. They obviously knew something I didn't. "What is it?"

"His dad?"

"That's what he said. Why?"

"It must have been a long distance call," quipped O'Neal.

"Why?" I asked again, bewildered.

"Don Elliott died over a year ago," answered Walker.

"Died? Dead!"

"A car crash left him paralysed from the waist down. Ronnie had to wash, dress and feed him. It ruined his business, he could never leave his side and Don knew it. That's why Ronnie found he'd taken an overdose. Ronnie had only popped out to the shops, but Don never made it to the hospital."

I felt worse than ever.

The ambulance reached the top of the hill and the siren began to screech as it edged into the traffic. I pictured Ronnie feeding his dad, buttoning up his shirt, watching over him as he slept and I wanted to say sorry.

The ambulance disappeared.

Walker turned to light his cigar, but before he could take the first puff it started to rain. A slow, soft drizzle. We all looked up.

"Come on," grunted Walker, leading us off the beach.

We headed for the shelter of Sea World and if there was an uglier building I had yet to see it. How something that looked like a reject from NASA was meant to blend in with a Norman castle and colourful chalets, I'll never know. The inside was modern, bland and featureless. We walked upstairs to the cafe and O'Neal ordered coffees.

We sat at a window seat and watched the rain drench the bay.

"So what do you know, Mahoney?" asked Walker.

"About what?"

"About anything?"

"I don't know anything about anything."

"You put yourself down, Mahoney."

"It's the only thing I'm good at."

Walker drank his coffee. It was so hot I couldn't even press it to my lips but he had practically finished before he spoke to me again.

"I'm going to let you in on a theory I have."

I tried to appear interested.

"Ronnie was working on a case, maybe you know, maybe you don't. The point is he saw or heard something he shouldn't have."

Walker finished his coffee. "You might want to think about what that something was, Mahoney."

"I have no idea!"

"That's all very well, but whoever killed Ronnie might not be so sure of it."

Walker stood up and looked at O'Neal. The Sergeant took a couple of quick sips and stood up to leave. Walker looked down at me.

"It's my guess that sooner or later somebody's going to come looking for some answers."

"I don't have any!"

"But that might not be good enough, Mahoney!"

~

I drove back to the office wondering what Ronnie had seen or heard that had got him killed. One minute he was telling me nothing ever happened, the next he was diving head first into the icy depths of the North Sea. Whatever it was, I needed to know and I needed to know now, just in case a man holding a baseball bat came looking for some answers.

I parked outside the office and got out of the car. It was only then that I noticed the bright red sports car come to a halt fifty yards away. I might not have given it another thought had the driver not appeared suspicious. He quickly jerked out of sight but I'd already noticed his silly black pork-pie hat, the kind reporters used to wear in old movies with 'press' cards tucked into the brim.

I deliberately ignored him and headed for the office.

The building was quiet and empty and the lights were out. I closed the street door and listened to the wind whistling in through a gap in the side window.

I went upstairs and fumbled through my pockets for the office key. I needn't have bothered. The door was open. My first thought was that Ronnie had returned. Then I remembered the stiff lying on a stretcher, and shuddered. It couldn't have been Ronnie.

I pushed on the glass panel with a finger and the door slowly creaked open. It threatened to take forever so I kicked back the door and the office snapped into view. It was a mess. The drawers of the filing cabinet had been left open and there was paperwork strewn all over the floor.

The door slammed against the wall making me jump. Another letter fell to the floor.

"Anybody here?"

Nothing and no one. I was grateful . . .

I turned to view the rest of the office just as an arm reached out towards me. I ducked and something smashed against the wall. Tiny pieces of china shattered all around me. I straightened up and caught a fist on the chin. My arms whirled like windmill sails caught in a gale as I staggered backwards across the room. I saw a figure standing in the middle of the room, then a wall, the ceiling, and the back of my head hit something hard . . .

~

I came round to greet a pair of beautiful brown eyes. They were staring into mine with an anxious expression. They could have belonged to an angel.

71

My head hurt like hell. Walker had been right. Whoever had bumped off Ronnie had caught up with me and tried to lay me to rest too. Now I was in heaven and it had all been so swift.

"Are you all right?" the angel with the brown eyes whispered.

I nodded and smiled and turned to see what heaven was really like. But I was confused. There were no harps, no clouds, just an empty chair and a dripping tap. I touched my head. It was bleeding. Why was death just as painful as life?

"Am I in heaven?"

"No. Scarborough. Ronnie Elliott's office to be exact. Don't you remember?"

I was sprawled on the floor. I sat up, slowly.

The angel's eyes belonged to Mandy, the girl from Spillanes. She tucked her jacket behind my head and propped me up against the wall.

"What the hell happened?"

"I think you've had burglars."

"Burglars?"

"Yes. Look at this place. It's in a right state."

I got to my feet and staggered to the desk. Something was bothering me. Why would anyone want to rob a PI's office?

"Someone was here," I agreed. "But I don't think they were burglars."

"You don't? Why not?"

"Because whoever was here was looking for something in particular."

Mandy stood up. All of her. I mean, her legs were so long I thought she was never going to stop. Her hourglass figure was trapped so tightly in the short black skirt she was going to need a crowbar to undress.

She stepped towards me, sweeping a wave of hair out of her eyes. She did that a lot.

"It must be very important then . . . Whatever it was they were looking for, I mean."

"I wasn't so sure . . . until now."

I ran my fingers across my head again. A lump the size of a tennis ball was rising from my skull.

"Does it hurt?"

"Only when I breathe."

She went to the sink, ran a cloth under the tap, sat me on the edge of the desk and gently dabbed the wound.

I winced.

"Sorry," she whispered.

I bit my tongue when she tried it again and let myself drown in the smell of her perfume and the warmth of her breath as she pressed up close to the side of my face.

"So, did they get what they were looking for?"

I shook my head.

"But how can you be so sure? I mean the place is in such a mess."

"Because, what they're looking for isn't here!"

She dabbed my wound a couple more times and then stepped back to look at me. "I think you'll live."

"Is that a promise?"

She went to the sink and rinsed out the cloth. It was only when she caught my gaze in the mirror that she asked, "What?"

"I was just wondering why you were here."

She shrugged. "Do I need a reason?"

"No." I smiled. "I was just curious."

"I work down the hall."

"You do?"

She waved a hand towards the door but it didn't help.

"In the office," she explained.

"You're Woodhall?" I asked.

"Yes, Mandy Woodhall."

I rolled up my lip. "I'm impressed."

"Why?"

"Do I have to have a reason?"

She smiled.

"I heard a noise. At first I didn't think much of it but when it went quiet I wondered if maybe Ronnie had fallen over or something."

"Did you know him well?"

"Not really. I mean, we'd pass one another on the stairs and talk about the weather and sometimes he'd treat me to pizza, or a Chinese. He thought I worked too hard and didn't eat enough."

"Did he ever discuss his business?"

"No, not really. He always said how nothing ever really happens here. Why'd you ask?"

I wondered how to say what I had to say. Unfortunately, when it came to handing out tact, I was at the back of the queue.

"He's dead."

"Dead?" she echoed softly.

"Yeah. He drowned. I've just seen them fish him out of the sea."

I watched her place a hand to her mouth, and listened to the hum of the street as it filled the office. Here I was, in a room with an angel, with no glad tidings of great joy.

"Are you all right?" I asked.

She nodded and stepped to the window to look outside. I thought about asking if she wanted a drink, a whisky. Or maybe even a hug. Then she turned as if she had something to say, but couldn't bring herself to say it.

"What is it?"

She looked away.

"Do you know something?"

"About what?"

"About anything."

Mandy glanced at me suspiciously. "Why'd you ask?"

"It's just that, if you want to know the truth, I don't think it was an accident . . ."

She was looking at me like a kid who'd been caught stealing from the corner shop.

"It's just that I . . ."

Her sentence trailed off as she turned back to the window.

I stepped up close to her. "That you what?"

"A little while ago I surveyed a hotel over on the south cliff. They were looking to extend the building. Unfortunately the land was unsafe. The rock formation was far too loose. It wouldn't have been safe to sink foundations, let alone build on."

"And?"

"About the same time a company from Leeds started to build a Victorian Village theme park affair on the land right below where I'd been surveying."

"I know it, in the old south bay pool area?"

"Yes. Purely in the interests of safety, you understand, I tried to get hold of somebody to tell them what I'd found. But nobody would talk to me. I wrote a letter to the council and one to the local paper. I simply assumed something would be done."

"But it wasn't."

Mandy looked like somebody had just spat in her face.

"I didn't know they'd carried on until after the hotel had collapsed. I couldn't believe it. So I asked Ronnie if he could look into it, you know, make some general enquiries to see if anyone had even taken notice of my letters . . ."

"What did you have in mind?"

"Why they'd gone ahead with construction when it was clearly unsafe."

"Sometimes money talks."

"Perhaps, but anyway, Ronnie thought he was on to something."

"Did he say what?"

She shook her head.

I sat on the edge of the desk and contemplated what she'd told me.

"I'm going to have to ask around. Somebody has to know something."

Mandy flicked hair out of her eyes again and stepped towards me. She was concerned.

"Are you going to be all right?"

"That depends on what you have in mind." I said, wondering if I should get off the desk.

She parted my knees with her hands and pressed her thighs hard against mine. Her perfume danced the tango on my cheek. I was shocked, happy and delirious, all at the same time. I knew Marlowe wouldn't approve, and that it would probably lead to a whole load of trouble, but I didn't care. Right now I was happy to go with the flow and battle the consequences as and when they arrived.

"Here's a clue." She cupped my face in her hands and I felt her tongue probe my lips and then the inside of my willing mouth. She pulled away, looked at me and whispered, "You'll be surprised how nice this can be."

We kissed again. Our lips danced, our tongues hugged and our hearts raced. I was in heaven in Ronnie Elliott's office. But it was all too brief, and then she was gone.

I walked across to the window. Outside the man in the hat had gone, so had his car. I was disappointed. For almost an hour I'd lived with the illusion of being someone important enough to be followed, when all the time it was nothing more than a man in a silly hat . . .

12

There are people who stride along the kerb, living life on the edge, excited by passing dangers. They are set apart from those who shuffle close to the wall, those anxious to get where they are going without too much fuss or attention. The rest of us walk somewhere in between, neither noticed nor caring, just part of the crowd, one of the many.

Then there are detectives, like Richard Mahoney, those who have to adapt to each new situation. Forced to mingle with the crowd and appear like everyone else, yet prepared to disappear into the shadows, unseen and unheard, or dart into the open to confront danger at a moment's notice. It was what paid the bills - taking the steps no one else would take.

That's what was going through my mind as I walked to the police station, mingling with the crowd. I didn't fancy life on the edge, especially if it meant getting myself killed. But at the same time I didn't want to hide in the shadows. I needed help. I needed Walker's help.

It was time to tell him about the negatives. He wouldn't be happy. I had stolen possible evidence and that would be enough for O'Neal to want to put me inside and throw away the key. But I knew it would grab their attention.

The station was a five-minute walk away, at the top end of the town, and it was then that I noticed 'him' again, the man in the silly black hat. He was some way behind me, knelt tying a shoelace and looking anything but inconspicuous.

It was one of the perfect ingredients to a good novel. Detectives were always followed, it added to the intrigue and made the reader want to know who and why. I wanted to know who and why. Was he a good guy, or a bad guy? Was he nervous about approaching me, or waiting for the right moment to teach me a lesson?

He was carrying a paper. Every now and again he pressed it to his face or glanced up at a building as if it were about to fall on him. I led him a merry dance, down side-streets paved with litter and graffiti, and through the town centre busy with holidaymakers and workers rushing to lunch.

And for a while he went along for the ride. For a while he was eager to tag along. Every so often I'd see his reflection in a shop window, or catch a glimpse of his hat out of the corner of my eye. But nothing happened. He never closed the gap, never approached me.

Finally I grew bored and headed once more for the police station.

I pulled open the door and glanced back down the street. The man in the hat had vanished. Maybe it had all been coincidence, my mind playing tricks on me. Or perhaps he'd got whatever it was he'd been looking for. Or maybe he just hadn't liked where I was heading . . .

The station was like nothing I'd seen on TV. It was a big grey shoe box of a building with large plate-glass windows that soaked up the sun and spat out the rain. There were no pimps or hookers being dragged from room to room like sacks of potatoes, no weary-eyed coppers scowling over endless piles of paperwork. No yelling, no screaming. All I could see was a policeman in a smartly pressed uniform leaning against the counter doing a lot of pointing and talking whilst another policeman sat opposite doing a lot of sighing and writing.

They were deliberating over a woman standing with a child in her arms. The kid looked over her shoulder at me. He was tired, his mouth covered in chocolate, or mud. I wasn't sure which and I had no intention of getting close enough to find out.

I winked, but he just kept staring, far beyond where I stood, and out at something warm and friendly and a million miles away from where he was now.

The woman was being charged with shop-lifting. There was a plastic carrier on the counter with bottles and freshly wrapped joints of meat. They didn't like what she'd done. They told her what a bad example she was setting her son.

The Sergeant wound up his report by banging a full stop with his pencil. It made the woman jump. It made everyone jump. She was led away through a door with the kid now fast asleep in her arms. His daydreams were over, but the nightmare had only just begun.

I had to wait for the Sergeant to file the report, sharpen his pencil, take out a handkerchief, blow his nose, fold away the handkerchief and order a coffee. I was about to say something when he raised an eyebrow in my direction.

"Can I help you?"

"I'd like to see Inspector Walker."

He whipped out his handkerchief again, clamped it to his face and sneezed.

"Bless you!" I replied - with a brick - I thought.

He grunted his thanks and neatly folded away the handkerchief.

"Is he expecting you?"

"No. I thought I'd surprise him."

The Sergeant's coffee arrived in a plastic cup. I tried to appear as if he wasn't bothering me, but it wasn't easy. He cleared his throat and pressed a buzzer. A door clicked open to my left and he nodded his head in the direction of the ceiling.

"Third floor. Ask someone when you get up there."

I couldn't conceal the smile on my face as he sneezed again and sent the coffee all over his shirt. Justice had been served.

Walker's office was nothing unusual. It was neat and tidy and smelled of cigar smoke. Although every window had been opened the heat was still oppressive.

He glanced up from a file and gave me the kind of look reserved for Jehovah's Witnesses. His face was covered with beads of perspiration and his tie hung loose around an unbuttoned collar. He wasn't having a good day. That made two of us.

He dropped his eyes back to the file as I pulled up a chair and made myself comfortable.

"Haven't you got anything better to do than to come and annoy me?" he sighed.

"I'm not sure there is anything better than annoying you."

Walker leaned forward and shuffled the paperwork back into the file.

"Well as you can see . . ."

"Have you found out who killed Ronnie Elliott yet?"

He wiped his brow with a handkerchief, stood and dropped the file into an open drawer. He remained standing and gazed out of the window.

"Nobody killed Ronnie Elliott," he said, matter-of-factly. "Nobody killed Ronnie Elliott, because Ronnie Elliott committed suicide."

"Suicide!" I balked. "Where the hell do you get 'suicide' from?"

Walker didn't answer.

"For Christ's sake, Inspector, it was only yesterday you were suggesting that the guy had been murdered!"

The word 'murdered' echoed around the room as the door opened.

"Murdered? Who on earth's been murdered, Inspector?"

Walker forced a smile and waved an arm in my direction.

"This is Mr Mahoney, sir. He was Ronnie Elliott's partner. I was just explaining . . ."

"Ronnie Elliott? Oh, yes. I knew his father."

Walker looked uncomfortable. "This is Superintendent Matthews. He headed the investigation."

Superintendent Matthews shook my hand. He had one of those annoying smiles, the kind that suggested he was the nicest guy you could ever wish to meet, while all the time you knew full well you couldn't trust him with the change in your pocket. He wore a three-piece suit and silver-rimmed glasses. Neither went with the polka-dot bow tie or the parting in his hair that would have had Moses leaping with joy.

"What makes you think it was suicide?" I asked.

Matthews smiled and perched on the edge of Walker's desk. His voice was calm. "We searched Elliott's house and found a note. Business was bad and he had gambling debts. They'd got out of control. Obviously it was too much for him."

I was looking at Walker but he was staring out of the window and said nothing.

"What about that lump on his head?" I snapped. "And the marks on his wrists?"

"He'd tied tubing around them when he'd injected morphine. We found traces of it in his blood. When that failed, he did the next best thing . . ."

"You call jumping into the sea the next best thing?"

"We have a witness who saw him jump. The currents are very strong. It would only have taken a matter of seconds. As for the bump on his head, he was smashed around on the rocks all night."

I sat there without saying anything and ran a finger around the inside of my collar. I wanted to know why Walker was so quiet. Why was he ready to let Matthews wrap everything up in little pink ribbons?

Matthews placed a report on Walker's desk, told me how sorry he was and left.

The heat was getting to me. My shirt clung to my skin, but I didn't feel half as uncomfortable as Walker looked.

"You don't seriously believe all that crap, do you?"

The Inspector half turned towards me and hunched his shoulders.

"You saw Elliott," I said. "And you know damn well he didn't commit suicide!"

Walker inched up his tie and sat back. I watched him fumble through the scattered paperwork for another cigar. His face was drawn. His eyes glazed. He had a different expression for every hour of the day.

I pressed my fingertips into the desk and yelled into his face, "What the hell's up with you? I thought you cared!"

He lit the cigar and took a deep breath. "I can't argue with the facts, Mahoney."

"Facts! What facts?"

"They're all we have and it's right there in the report."

I looked at the paperwork on his desk, but it didn't mean a thing to me. "So what about instinct?"

"What about proof?" he countered. "Where's the proof, Mahoney?"

That was it, the knockout blow, the uppercut that sent me spinning to the canvas. I had nothing to respond with. Walker was playing by the rules. That was his job. He had to, because without them he didn't have a job and there would be chaos and anarchy. I slumped into my chair.

"What is it with you?" I asked.

He wiped his brow and picked up a photo from the desk, studying it like it was the first time he'd laid eyes on it.

"You want to know something?" he asked.

"Will it help?"

He tapped the photo with a fingertip. "I'm one of the few people in this department who actually looks forward to going home at night, because

I'm one of the few people here lucky enough to have a family who enjoy seeing him come home."

"Lucky you!"

"It's not just a matter of luck, you idiot! It's knowing when to draw the line and I know when to draw it."

Walker placed the photo back on the desk. I could see it was a picture of him standing next to an attractive woman and two young girls. They were all smiling at the camera, even Walker.

"When I joined the force I was just like O'Neal. I worked all the hours God sent and then some. I wanted to make the streets safe. I wanted to put the world to rights . . . but the truth is that no matter how hard I tried, it was never enough."

"So now you just put in time and head off home, even if it means somebody getting away with murder?"

He slammed a fist onto the desk. Ash from the cigar flew everywhere.

"Don't push it, Mahoney! Don't push it."

I looked at him and smiled. "You can't kid me, Walker, 'cause I've seen the film, you remember, the one where the authorities keep things quiet about the man-eating shark because it'll be bad for business. So they pretend it doesn't exist and hope that it'll just go away. Trouble was, they forgot to tell the shark and it just went on eating people till eventually they were forced to do something about it. The question is, Inspector, how many people are going to die before you do something?"

I was half expecting Walker to blow a fuse. But he didn't. To my surprise he leaned back in his chair and smiled, not like the smile in the photo, but more of a smirk. It puzzled me.

"I know what this is all about, Mahoney."

"You do?"

"Let me tell you something, I've worked in this town for over a decade without seeing so much as a drunken brawl. Then one day you come along claiming to have found bodies all over the place . . ."

"Are you suggesting I'm making it up?"

"Look at it this way. If nothing happens all week, I still get paid, that's my perk. But people like you and Ronnie Elliott, they eventually go out of business. You know what I'm saying?"

I shot to my feet and glared at him. I couldn't get to the door fast enough.

"You're like a reporter, Mahoney. Without a good story you're a nobody with nothing."

I was desperate to say something. To retort with a line that would have had Walker eating his words. But I couldn't think of anything. All I could do was look angry, slam the door and leave.

A cold wind swept down the street and slapped me across the face. But it had nothing to do with the weather. Reality had paid me a fleeting visit. If it had been a dream, it would have been a bad dream. I saw myself drowning in a pool of water, surrounded by bodies, money and negatives. Meanwhile Walker sat in a chair, smoking a cigar and tapping a lifebelt as if playing a drum. I promised to 'come clean' and tell him all I knew. Just as he was about to throw me the lifebelt his wife appeared and his children ran happily towards him. He greeted them with open arms and left me choking, spitting, gargling and cursing his name with my dying breath.

~

My head was so full of questions there wasn't any room for the answers. I felt aggrieved because this wasn't just about Ronnie Elliott, Colin Fitzsimmons and the girl any more, it was about me and my sanity. Someone had played me for a fool.

I went back to the car and headed off towards Helen Fitzsimmons' house. The money she'd paid me was burning a hole in my conscience. If I was to live the life of a PI then I needed to keep my morals intact. I had to be a man of honour, a knight with touches of sainthood, a detective with a sense of obligation, not someone who was bought off with a pocketful of loose change and a honeypot smile. But I got so worked up about giving her a piece of my mind that it was a good ten minutes before the rest of my mind realised that I had no idea where she lived. But somebody else had to, people with her kind of wealth couldn't live in secrecy in a place like this.

My 'guide' turned out to be a middle-aged man walking his dog. Yes, he knew of Mrs Fitzsimmons and yes, he knew where she lived. Didn't everyone? I told him I was new in town. She lived with her father, Mr Laughton. He pointed, motioning left and right and then left again and instructed me to follow Belvedere Avenue as far as it went and I couldn't miss the house. All the time he looked at me like he wouldn't trust me to see him across the road. It was a look I'd seen before. It was the look the locals gave every passing stranger who stumbled into town asking where a certain Count Dracula resided . . .

I took a left onto Belvedere Avenue and followed the road as it curved round, high above the south bay. The area was a rich mix of private homes and expensive guest houses. Away to my right the cliff face fell sharply to the sea.

The Laughton house was the last building on the right. A Tudor-style home set so far back into its green surroundings that I fully expected to be ambushed by natives as I pulled into the driveway.

Tall iron gates blocked my way. They were no longer impressive and I noted the rust poking through the thin, peeling paint.

I left the car on the road and set off down the drive on foot, the gravel crunching beneath my feet like crisp morning snow. I felt hot and sticky. There wasn't so much as a breeze, it was like stepping into a greenhouse. I loosened my tie and noticed how the acres of lawn lay uncut, the untended flower borders overgrown with weeds that grew like stubble.

I finally reached a door big enough to accept an entire congregation and pulled back the head of a large brass knocker. It thudded against the solid mahogany.

There was no reply.

I tried again, a little louder.

A few seconds later an elderly woman with grey, closely cropped-hair and a hint of make-up opened the door and appraised me through slitted eyes.

"Er, my name's Richard Mahoney. I'm a Private Investigator." I couldn't believe how easily the words rolled off my tongue. "I've been doing some work for Helen, Mrs Fitzsimmons. I was wondering . . . is she home?"

The woman appeared uncomfortable. "Do you have a card?"

Hell! No, I didn't have a card. People just didn't ask for cards any more.

"I . . . er . . ." But whatever excuse I was about to come up with died on my lips with the booming voice that echoed past the old woman and straight into my eardrums.

"Who is it, Mary?"

The old woman turned. "A Mr Mahoney. He claims to be a detective, or something, says he's been working for Helen . . ."

"Well, don't just stand there, woman. Show him in!"

Mary inched back and motioned for me to enter.

There, as large as life, was Roger Laughton. I recognised him from the photos I'd seen in the papers, none of which had done him credit. His thick wavy hair, strong chin and flat stomach defied his sixty years. He had made a lot of money but you would never have guessed it. His blue suit was the kind you could pick blindfold from a rack at Oxfam and it looked like he'd been wearing it for weeks. What he lacked in exhibition he made up for in confidence as he strode towards me with a smile wide enough to hang a clothes line on.

"Mr McNulty. Nice to meet you. My name's Roger Laughton. I'm Helen's father."

Laughton was cheerful, too cheerful for this time of day, or for any other time. He took my hand and shook it like he expected a ton of apples to fall from my head.

"Can I take your coat?" the old woman asked.

"This is the wife, Mary."

"Mrs Laughton," I smiled.

"Your coat?" she said again.

"Er, yeah, thanks." I couldn't help thinking how sad she appeared. She looked up at her husband. "Don't forget your medicine."

He waved a hand like it didn't matter and we stood and watched Mary disappear with my coat.

"Perhaps we could have some tea, Mary?" he called after her.

She turned and looked at me with something of a plea not to put her to any trouble.

"Er, not for me thanks," I obliged.

"Perhaps something stronger then," said Laughton, wrapping an arm around my shoulders and leading me down the hall.

"So, you're a detective!" he said, excitedly.

"Yes."

"How fascinating!"

"Sometimes."

"But dangerous?"

"Occasionally."

We reached a pair of double doors which creaked open as Laughton pushed on them. We stepped together into a very large room. The walls stretched as far as the eye could see, and the ceiling disappeared into the sky. It was as cold as hell and the most untidy room I'd ever seen. There was a desk strewn with paperwork and an old-fashioned typewriter. There were cardboard boxes and piles of newspapers against the wall. Rows of books of every size and colour lined the shelved walls. Most of the antique furniture was covered in dust sheets and it smelt like the place had never benefited from a breath of fresh air.

Laughton closed the doors behind us, whilst I made the mistake of appearing interested in one of two flowerpots standing guard by the doors. The old man seized the opportunity.

"Do you collect antiques, Mr McNulty?"

"Only bills!"

"Have you any idea what these are?" he said motioning to the flowerpots.

"Something you put flowers in?"

"Flowers? Mr McNulty!" He looked at me like I'd broken wind.

"Actually, it's Mahoney!"

"Oh, goodness me no!" he laughed aloud. "It's seventeenth century china. Worth close to two thousand pounds each."

"Yeah, well I did mean real ones . . ."

"Obviously you don't care for antiques!"

"They're okay if you like living in the past," I muttered.

"And you don't . . . like living in the past, I mean?"

"What's the point? I can't do anything about it."

"But can you do anything about the future?"

"Why bother waking up if I can't?"

Laughton studied me for a moment as he wiped his glasses with a handkerchief. Then he pointed me in the direction of a nearby chair. I sat down and wrapped my hands over the arms of the seat, in case I got sucked down into the floorboards.

The old man made his way to a cabinet shaped like the prow of a ship. He flicked a switch. The light flickered and died.

"Damn thing," he mumbled. "Must get it fixed. Er, would you care for a drink, Mr McNulty?" Things were looking up.

"Please, call me Richard," I sighed.

"A whisky perhaps?"

"You obviously read a lot of detective novels."

He smiled, then fixed an embarrassed gaze on me. "Oh, I'm sorry. That was rather presumptuous of me, wasn't it?"

"Could I just have a beer?"

"Of course."

"I don't use it much myself," he said tapping the drinks cabinet. "It was Helen's idea, but every now and again I feel like a treat."

Laughton handed me a bottle, poured himself a brandy and settled into the chair opposite me. It was obvious he was neither comfortable nor relaxed. When he wasn't glancing at his watch he was peering at the clock on the wall and fighting with an expression which suggested he needed to be somewhere else.

"Helen isn't in I'm afraid."

"Oh," I said, suddenly wondering how I was going to pass the time of day with Laughton while I drank the beer.

But he had plans. He uncrossed his legs and leant towards me. He spoke eagerly in nothing more than a whisper.

"I suppose you're wondering why I invited you in?"

"It had crossed my mind."

"I'm a little curious," he smiled. "You see, I've met a lot of different people in my time, but never a Private Investigator."

He worked his small green eyes over me like I was a prized specimen in one of his collections; something for him to ogle at, an idle curiosity. It made me uncomfortable.

"I hate to disappoint you, Mr Laughton, but I'm afraid Private Investigators are just like everybody else."

In fact, this particular PI was more like everybody else than he cared to admit.

It failed to dampen his enthusiasm. He sat back.

"But it must be fun, fighting criminals, chasing cars and enjoying the company of beautiful and glamorous women?" he added with a wink.

I forced a smile. I just couldn't be bothered with all the lies. I also got the impression that, deep down, he didn't really give a damn about PIs. He was trying to be clever. He was driving around in circles whilst all the time wanting to know why his daughter had hired me.

He sipped the brandy. "Maybe there's something I can do for you?"

I raised an eyebrow.

"I mean, I'd hate you to have had a wasted journey."

"I enjoyed the ride."

Laughton pressed his lips tight and tapped his fingers on the arm of the chair.

"Actually there is something you can do for me," I told him.

"Oh!"

I put the bottle on a side table and rummaged inside my jacket pockets. He watched with interest as I pulled out an envelope.

"I was wondering if you'd give this to Helen."

Laughton took the envelope and held it in his hand.

"It's some money she gave me the other day."

"Is there a problem with it?"

"She overpaid."

A faint smile brushed across his face and wiped away any lingering suspicions he might have had.

"I'm afraid generosity has always been one of Helen's weaknesses."

"Weaknesses?"

"It comes with having everything handed to her on a plate I'm afraid."

"According to Helen, she's very independent."

The old man smiled. "Is that what she told you?"

I nodded.

"Because of course she has no idea."

"That makes two of us."

"I've helped her, Mr McNulty. All along and quietly of course, made a call here and another there, put a few contacts her way. I've always been there for her."

"And it never occurred to you that she might have been able to do it anyway? Or couldn't you handle her being successful without your help?"

Laughton got to his feet without saying a word. He stepped to a shelf and picked out a large, red, leather-bound book. It was bigger than a cathedral bible. While he fussed with the pages I returned to my beer and stared out of the large bay windows. It was an incredible view. Miles and miles of lawns, weeping willows and withering flowers right up to the edge of the cliff that gave way to the deep blue of the sea beyond. It was a view I could never grow tired of.

"Have you ever heard of The Merchant of Venice, Mr McNulty?"

"Is that the one were someone tries to make burgers out of an old friend?"

Laughton lowered his head and glanced at me over the rim of his glasses. I doubted he discussed classics with the plebeians very often.

"Crudely put, but correct. However, it's the sub-plot that appeals to me. It concerns the plight of a young lady by the name of Portia who is left a very large inheritance by her father . . ."

"Lucky girl."

"You might think so," he said, pacing back and forth across the floor. "But, as it happens, even when the girl's father passes away, he still controls her life."

"How?" I asked, trying to appear intrigued.

"It is a requirement of his will that Portia must marry before she can receive the inheritance."

"Yeah!"

"You see, Shakespeare was merely reflecting the concerns of many fathers who are anxious about leaving money to their daughters. In those days, of course, women were regarded as irresponsible, reckless, spendthrifts. Therefore it was vital they married a man who could bring stability and order to their lives."

He came to a halt in front of the window. He was blocking my view and drooling over the book.

I finished my beer and stood up. It was time to leave.

Laughton snapped the book shut. "You don't agree?"

I tugged on my ear and wondered what the hell any of what he was rambling on about had to do with me. "I'd have thought spendthrifts came in all shapes and sexes!"

Laughton placed the book back on the shelf and let out a soft, defeated sigh. "My daughter thinks I'm old fashioned. She also thinks I'm sexist. Sexist!" he laughed. "There was no such word when I was young."

"That doesn't mean to say it didn't exist."

"So you agree with her?"

"It's none of my business."

He smiled and walked over to where I stood. "You don't like me do you, Mr McNulty?"

No I didn't. But I wasn't about to admit it. Besides, I couldn't see that it made any difference one way or another.

"Oh, I know it's nothing personal. You just don't like what I stand for, do you?" He took off his glasses and started to wipe them again with his handkerchief. "When I arrived in this town, Mr McNulty, all I had was the small change in my pocket. Nobody looked out for me. I had to take any work that was going, and I did. I worked all day and all night and saved every penny until I was able to buy my own business. I went from strength to strength simply because I knew the value of money. I'd like Helen to do the same. Unfortunately generosity never made a fortune, don't you agree?"

The old man looked at me and replaced his glasses. They shone in the afternoon light and I could see the window reflected in the lenses.

I handed him the empty bottle. "Personally, I'd rather sleep at night."

"You would?" he sounded surprised and looked at me as if it was a crime.

"Yeah, I would."

We made polite conversation about the weather as he walked me to the gates. Then he told me not to worry about the money. He tried to get me to keep it. I stubbornly refused to take it back. I was about to leave when he went quiet and started to run his foot back and forth across the gravel. He wanted to ask me something, but obviously didn't know how.

"Look," he said eventually. "I don't know how these things usually work. I've never had to pay anyone to sort out my problems before, and no doubt you will tell me it's none of my business . . . but is my daughter in trouble?"

It was a strange question for a caring father to ask a stranger.

"To be honest, Mr Laughton, I'm not really sure." That was the truth, after all.

"So why would she hire you?"

I shrugged. "She has her reasons."

"Name one!"

I tried to sound polite. "I'm sorry, but you're going to have to ask her."

He looked troubled. The line he was carving in the gravel grew deeper. Deep enough to fall into.

"Don't think I haven't tried. Unfortunately Helen can be very stubborn at times."

"Another one of her weaknesses, perhaps!"

Laughton looked at me long and hard and there wasn't a compassionate line on his face. "Don't play games with me, young man!"

"Then don't ask me what I don't know!"

He started to cough. He didn't sound so good.

"I think it's time for your medicine."

I turned to leave and he grabbed my arm and held it tight. His grip was firm and strong. It wasn't the kind of grip I would have associated with someone who'd pushed pens most of his life.

His eyes narrowed. "Then I'll be blunt, McNulty. If anything happens to Helen, I'm going to hold you personally responsible."

13

The town baked and shimmered in the afternoon heat. The sun sizzled, the tarmac boiled and everybody headed for the foreshore. The cars were bumper to bumper, the day-trippers nose to nose and the beach was packed with people of all shapes and sizes sitting in brightly-coloured deckchairs, sacrificing their pale white skin under knotted handkerchiefs while children screamed, dogs barked and the crash of waves disappeared into the distance.

With time to kill, I parked the car at the bottom of Belvedere Avenue and made my way towards the beach through the nearby 'Italian' gardens where old people huddled together on a row of green benches, chewing cucumber sandwiches and admiring the view across the bay.

A narrow path led me left and then right at forty-five degree angles through the perfumed scent of flowers and past bony grey trees bent like tortured statues in the cold sea air. I wanted to take a look at the outdoor pool to see what had caused Mandy so much distress, and the council so much discomfort. I came out just behind the refurbished Spa Theatre where the wealthy Victorians were once entertained or cured of melancholia, gout, rheumatic aches and pains and chronic flatulence. But the walls were silent now. All I could hear was the breaking of the tide and all I could feel was a sea breeze as it whipped up the stench of seaweed and human refuse from the graffiti riddled pillars below.

The old pool was blocked off. I peered through the wire fencing at the bare, cracked concrete. High above a fence, at the far end of the pool, concrete gave way to the accumulation of bricks, wood and detritus that had drifted down the cliff from the now defunct Gables. It was hard to imagine how anyone could make the place any uglier if they tried and nobody seemed in much of a rush to put things right again.

Feeling less than inspired I started back along the beach. I figured I needed a treat. I passed the Harbour Cafe. I was in luck, the place was practically empty. Everyone else seemed to want to take advantage of the sunshine and that was fine by me. I glanced up at the menu and certificates of excellence and plumped for a Chocolate Sundae with all the trimmings.

I took a seat near the window and viewed the rest of the interior from there. It had the appearance of an American-style diner. A long bright counter with bar stools and pretty young girls in mint aprons and matching hats. With the sun streaming through the windows it didn't seem a million miles away from California.

I imagined Marlowe sitting on one of the stools, ordering coffee and doughnuts. He looked tired and drawn from the endless hours of deliberation over another seemingly hopeless case. What would he make of this, I wondered? Which way would he turn next? Because I didn't have a clue.

The Sundae was about the best thing that had happened to me since arriving in the town. I was on my third spoonful when a shadow fell across the table and I looked up to see the man in the silly black hat staring back at me.

"Are you Mr Mahoney?" He asked.

"If I'm not, you've been following the wrong man all day."

"M-m-m-my name's Eddie, Eddie Hartless. I'm a journalist."

And with a name like that he was never destined to be anything else. He held out a hand. I ignored it and kept on eating.

"Can we talk?"

I thought about saying 'no'. I didn't like journalists, and I didn't much care for the way he'd been following me around, but before I could say anything Hartless had slumped into the seat opposite.

"I-I-I need to ask you something, Mr Mahoney."

"Go ahead and make it my starter for ten. My music's pretty good but I'm a bit rusty on politics!"

Hartless was nervous, that much I could tell. He ran his tongue along the inside of his cheek like he was chewing a spanner and pressed the tips of his fingers together till they turned white. He was staring at me from the corner of his eye.

"Why are the police covering up Ronnie Elliott's death?"

The question took me by surprise and I had a hell of a job trying not to show it.

"How should I know?"

"Because you've been talking to the police, to Inspector Walker."

"I also spoke to the girl behind the counter, but all I got was a chocolate sundae."

Hartless raised his chin ever so slightly and then slammed a fist onto the table.

Before I could respond he was up and halfway to the door.

I should have left it at that . . .

"If it bothers you that much, why don't you ask him yourself?"

But Hartless had been calling my bluff. He was sitting opposite me again before I had time to draw breath.

"I did, but I only got the same old runaround."

I sat back and looked at him hard. He appeared normal enough. He had features, characteristics, perhaps even friends and a family, and it was possible that if I talked to him long enough we might even have become friends. But at the back of my mind was the constant reminder that he was a low-life reporter who'd go to any lengths to get a story.

"So, what's Ronnie Elliott's death to you?" I asked.

Hartless pressed the palms of his hands to the table. "Ronnie was a sort of friend. I met him at the Casino. I was only a freelance back then. He introduced me to some people. It's largely thanks to Ronnie, and m-m-my talent, that I'm where I am t-t-today."

I let the sound of crashing waves and squaking gulls fill the room while I thought over what Hartless had said.

"Look," I said, pushing the ice-cream away. "I'd like to help, but I'm not sure there's a whole lot I can do. Like you said, I've been getting the runaround all week and I'm as much in the dark as you are."

"How about you t-t-tell me what Helen Fitzsimmons wanted with you."

He studiously avoided my gaze by staring out of the window.

"You are working for her, right?"

I waited for him to look at me. "How long have you been following me?"

"Long enough," he whispered. "D-D-Do you know what happened to her brother?"

"I didn't know she had a brother!"

"His name was Eric."

"And?"

"He drowned . . ."

"So?" I frowned. "Lots of people drown."

"In six inches of water? Do me a f-f-favour!"

Hartless had the smug look of having reeled me in. He had my attention and he knew it.

"And what's that got to do with Helen Fitzsimmons?"

Hartless glanced hungrily at what was left of the ice-cream. "Have you finished with that?"

I nodded.

He reached out for the spoon and I caught hold of his arm.

"I said, what's that got to do with Helen Fitzsimmons?"

Hartless shook his head. "I'm not sure. But she s-s-seems to have an awful lot of bad luck, don't you think!"

He spooned ice-cream into his mouth.

"She wanted to know why Ronnie was following her," I told him. After all, it was no big secret.

"Following her? I d-d-didn't know he was."

"Neither did I."

"So, what did you t-t-tell her?"

"That neither did I!"

Hartless grinned. At first I thought it was because he'd found the remark funny, but I was wrong.

"I th-th-thought you cared, Mahoney."

"Maybe I do. Maybe I just have a whole lot of trouble showing it."

"You don't t-t-trust me!"

"Give me one good reason why I should?"

"I can't. I mean I wouldn't t-t-trust anyone."

"Especially when, like you, they've taken so long to approach me!"

"I was nervous. I still am!"

"Of me?"

"They've just found a good friend of mine washed up on the beach and all he did was ask a f-f-few questions."

"The police said it was suicide."

"I know it wasn't."

"Yeah? How?" I got the impression Hartless was winding me up. Bugging me for answers that I didn't have, and he was doing the thing with his cheek again.

"Because he had to t-t-take care of his father and I know for a f-f-fact that he would never just abandon him . . ."

Now I had him.

"His old man? That's impossible. He died over a year ago."

Hartless stopped eating and stared at me like I'd gone mad. "Who t-t-told you that?"

"The police. Why?"

"Because I spoke to Ronnie's father the other night," he answered quietly.

"Are you sure?"

He nodded. "Positive. I've spoken t-t-to him lots of times. I'll give you his number if you like."

"But that doesn't make sense. Why would the police lie about a thing like that?"

Hartless didn't answer. Instead he reached into his inside pocket, all the time never taking his eyes off me. He spread a newspaper on the table so I could read it and turned to one of the inside pages. Below plans to convert a listed building into car park Hartless placed a finger. "Read that!"

> BODY FOUND IN SEA
> A man's body was yesterday found washed up on Skelton Mills beach. His identity has yet to be revealed. Meanwhile police continue to investigate the cause of death.

"But they know it was Ronnie!" I exclaimed.

"I know."

I pushed the paper back across the table and watched him put it back into his pocket.

"It doesn't make sense."

"There's a lot that doesn't make s-s-sense right now."

He had a point, but I wasn't going to let him see that I thought so.

"Is there anything else?"

Yes. There was, there was a whole lot more. But I wasn't sure how much to tell him. Eventually I opted for the bit that troubled me most, the bit about finding Colin Fitzsimmons dead on the floor. Hartless got excited and was too quick in reminding me about the girl. I looked at him and wondered if he was just reading my mind, or if he had inside information.

"How the hell did you know about her? The police never said anything!"

"Not officially anyway," he smirked. "Did you get a good look at her?"

Before I could answer he was fumbling through his pockets. He pulled out a photo and handed it to me. The girl in the snap was smiling and happy, with a dog in her lap.

"Is th-th-that her?"

I nodded.

"Her name's Tracey Staples. She works for the council. At least she did. She was sacked a few weeks ago. Rumour was sh-sh-she was seen taking photos of confidential documents."

"And how would you know that?"

"She was caught on security cameras. Nobody has seen or heard from her since."

"Maybe she's on holiday?"

Hartless sat back confidently. "But you know what you saw, don't you, Mr Mahoney?"

"So everybody keeps telling me."

"So!" Hartless was full of beans, his eyes popping, his hands shaking with excitement.

It was time to throw a spanner in his works.

"So, nothing, Hartless. All you've got is some paranoid rich girl, a PI who may have committed suicide and two dead bodies that got up and walked away."

"Tha-that seems like an awful lot to me!"

"Yeah, well maybe it's enough for tomorrow night's edition."

Hartless tucked his bottom lip into his waistband and narrowed his eyes.

"Is that what you think, that this is just another story?"

"It doesn't matter what I think. I'm just a nobody with nothing. I went to the police and they laughed me out of the station. Now I'm starting to think they did me a favour because, to be quite honest, I'm out of my league . . ."

"Well, then, thank you for your t-t-time, Mr Mahoney."

Hartless got to his feet, his forlorn expression only disturbed by his frantic tongue spinning around the inside of his cheek again.

"Hey look, I'm sorry, all right. I tried. But there's nothing I can do."

Hartless pulled down his hat and took a couple of steps towards the door. Then he stopped. "Would it help if I knew who Ronnie was meeting the night he . . ."

I didn't answer.

Hartless stepped closer. "Look, I don't blame you for not getting involved. Something's going on here, s-s-something dangerous and you have every right to walk away while you still can."

Hartless headed off towards the door . . . and this time I let him leave.

14

The man in the pale blue suit looked up at me and shook his head.

"I'm sorry, but Mr Hebden isn't in his office."

His name was Malcolm Lindley and he worked for the council. It wasn't a lucky guess, or fancy detective work on my part. I was standing in the council's depot, a former prison with an entrance flanked by gothic lodges, arrow-slits and drawbridge chains and Lindley's name was typed in large black letters on a badge pinned to his Bugs Bunny tie. He had the big round cheeks of an overfed hamster and short stumpy fingers that came from years of tapping keyboards.

"Then maybe you can tell me where he is, it's very important."

Lindley looked at me and then at his computer screen. "It's his day off."

"Why didn't you tell me that in the first place?"

"I forgot."

"Do you have any idea where I can find him?"

Lindley shook his head. He didn't want any trouble, and he didn't want to be any help either.

I gave him a look of contempt and headed for the door.

"When I finally meet up with Mr Hebden I'll let him know what a great help you were, Lindley. I'm sure he'll be impressed."

"You could . . ." he stopped to clear his throat, ". . . you could try the harbour."

I turned to watch him wipe sweat from his brow with a handkerchief. His eyes looked everywhere but not at me.

"He owns a boat. The Mayfair. You never know . . ." his voice tailed off.

It had crossed my mind to speak to Hebden shortly after meeting Hartless. He worked for the council so he might know something about Tracey Staples. It was a shot in the dark but at least it was me pulling the trigger for once.

I found the Mayfair. It was hooked up behind the Cutty Sark, the town's pride and joy - a sailing ship used for transporting visitors on trips around the twin bays.

From the moment Lindley had mentioned the word 'boat', I'd pictured a powerful craft that was capable of slicing through the waves, pulling a couple of water-skiers at breakneck speed, while bikini-clad women sipped cocktails on the back seat and let the sea breeze brush through their wavy locks and over their tanned, golden bodies.

What I found was a rotten wreck that I doubted could cut its way through melted butter. Hebden was polishing the rail that circled what passed for a deck and smiling a quiet, satisfied smile.

I looked at him and cleared my throat, loud enough to grab his attention.

He turned and offered me the kind of expression that suggested he couldn't quite put a name to the face.

"Mr Hebden?"

"Yes."

"It's me, Mahoney. I met you the other day. I was with Helen Fitzsimmons."

"Oh, that's right, the Private Investigator. How are you?"

"Fine. I was wondering if I could have a word?"

"Sure. Step aboard."

But he must have noted the look of fear in my eyes as I stared down at the gangplank swaying in front of me.

"Not got sea legs?"

"I find they bring out the diced carrot in me!"

"But we're in the harbour, Mr Mahoney!"

"It doesn't make any difference. I even get seasick on a rowing machine."

Hebden laughed. A shallow, painful laugh that scattered a flock of nearby gulls up towards the castle walls.

"Just take short steps and don't look down."

But that's exactly what I did, as my right foot left the harbour wall and my eyes drifted to the thick oil spilling colours of the rainbow into the dark, murky waters below.

Hebden reached out and took my arm, pulling me onto the deck. Instantly I could feel the floor swaying and my stomach heaved, longing for the stability of dry land.

"It's really not that bad."

"You try telling my stomach that."

"You really don't like the water!" he sounded surprised.

"If I was meant to be this close to water I'd have been born with webbed feet!"

Hebden stamped his foot onto the deck a couple of times. "This is a coble, Mr Mahoney. Its design is based on the Vikings' longships. It was a pretty efficient smuggling boat in its time. She's nineteen feet long with a single mast, a rudder four feet below the keel and most of the fishermen here will tell you that if they were trapped in a storm they'd rather be in one of these than a rubber lifeboat any day of the week."

I forced a smile. He was trying his best, unfortunately it wasn't good enough.

"Still not convinced?"

I shook my head.

"I have an idea."

I watched as Hebden disappeared down some steps leaving me alone with the creak of timber, the smack of the waves and the smell of fish in the damp salt air. He returned a minute later holding two mugs.

"Here, try this."

I took one and looked at him.

"Go on. It'll do you good."

I took a sip.

"It tastes like coffee."

"That's because it is coffee."

But there was an aftertaste that left me feeling like I'd swallowed a lump of coal.

"The aftertaste you're experiencing is an ingredient that was passed down to me by my old man. It settles your stomach. Give it a minute or two."

Hebden pulled up a couple of old crates and we sat down. The taste of coal was working its way down my throat, but I still felt like every ounce of blood had been drained from my body.

I watched Hebden drink his coffee. He was wearing a smart shirt and smart trousers and somehow he didn't look like someone who belonged on a boat.

"So what's with the boat?" I asked.

Hebden smiled. "It belonged to my old man, and his old man before him. The difference is it meant something then. People could earn a living because the harbour had an armada then, not just the odd boat"

"And now?"

"Now, I just use it to get away from the office. I like it here, Mr Mahoney. I like to look up at the castle and the cottages and imagine how it used to be when people worked for one another."

"And if anybody ever put a brick through a window?"

"I'm sorry?"

"Nothing, just something I heard the other day about people looking out for one another."

"It's true, nobody cares any more. The whole town is just going to waste."

There was a far-off look in his eye. A sad look. The kind of look you didn't want to see too often.

"Are things really that bad?"

Hebden looked at me for a moment.

"You're not from round here are you, Mr Mahoney?"

"No, but I used to come here with my parents."

"But not any more?"

"I think I've outgrown them now!"

But Hebden was too lost in thought to hear what I'd said.

"You wouldn't believe what I once had planned for this town, Mr Mahoney."

He got to his feet and stretched his limbs. He was staring out through a forest of masts at the amusement arcades beyond. "The problem is nobody seems to know where to take the town next. Some prefer a more traditional resort, with beautiful gardens and parks and small shops and quaint cafes; others feel we should become more like Blackpool and build theme parks with slides and laser light shows."

"And in the meantime?"

"In the meantime, people don't come back and the whole town goes to waste."

"And then there's the other problem, of course."

Hebden frowned. "What other problem?"

"I was speaking to Mandy Woodhall. She's a local surveyor. She was telling me about the site down by the old pool. They were planning some Victorian theme park down there which she was convinced wasn't safe."

Hedbden looked out towards where The Gables had once stood and then down below it to where the fenced-off remains of the old pool still littered the coastline. He appeared sad. "I didn't know about that," he said softly. "Such a terrible waste. But then again, if we don't try something we're accused of doing nothing."

A cold wind whipped in off the sea. I decided it was time to leave. I thanked him for the coffee and his time. He smiled and told me any time, and I got the feeling he meant it.

"So how do you feel now?" he asked.

"Better," I had to admit.

Hebden smiled.

"When you get some time I'll show you what really makes this town special, Mr Mahoney."

"Yeah, I'd like that." I turned to face the gangplank and it was only then that I remembered what it was I had wanted to ask Hebden about. "Oh, I was wondering, have you ever heard of Tracey Staples?"

Hebden looked at me, then at the deck, then back at me. He shook his head. "No, why?"

"She used to work for the council."

"I'm sure there are a lot of people who 'used' to work for the council, Mr Mahoney."

"Yeah, but she was fired a few weeks ago for taking pictures of confidential documents."

Hebden appeared to think for a moment but came up blank. "I'm sorry, the name doesn't ring a bell."

"Well, it was worth a try."

A storm was gathering on the horizon. It brought with it a cool breeze and had already turned the sea into a shade of foreboding grey. Powerful waves had started to lap against the harbour walls. Hebden appeared momentarily concerned.

"I'd better get packed away, Mr Mahoney, it looks like we're heading for a storm."

"Yeah well, thanks for everything."

"Any time."

I stepped eagerly onto dry land again.

A fishing boat chugged out of the shelter of the harbour towards the darkening sky.

I looked back at Hebden. He was staring across the bay at his beloved town. He appeared sad, let down. I wanted to tell him that everything was going to be all right, but I couldn't.

~

Apparently I was going through a bad time, but if I kept faith in my own ability then all would turn out well, even though it would not be exactly as I had planned.

Funny that, because I'd given up planning anything a long time ago. But that served me right for trying to find inspiration in a horoscope.

There was only one thing left to do. I had to swallow my pride and talk to Eddie Hartless. He was the only one on my side, or so it seemed. Maybe he really did care about Ronnie. Or perhaps he was just after a story. It didn't really matter any more, just as long as I got some answers.

Eddie was covering a story on the local Opera House. I drove straight there, intrigued to see what he could find worth writing about. Surely this would be an assignment that would stretch his creative abilities to the limit.

The Opera House was in a transitional period, it was going from bad to worse. It was hard to imagine that it had once played host to many of the country's major stars. Anybody who was anybody had appeared there at one time or another. But all that seemed such a long time ago as I looked up at the graffitied walls and smashed windows encased in a giant cobweb of scaffolding and green mesh. Even the front doors limped on their hinges as I pushed them open.

The lobby was cold and sparse, but nothing a lick of paint and a new carpet couldn't have put to rights. I walked up a ramp towards the stalls, pulled back a curtain and glanced up at the stained, plump seats that rose at a ninety degree angle away from the stage and towards jagged beams that gave way to stars and a half-moon.

Eddie was on stage shining a torch onto his notebook. I cleared my throat and caught his attention. He flashed the light my way.

"Oh, Mr Mahoney. No, please wait . . ."

But it was too late, I'd already taken a couple of steps and that was enough. I watched a tide of muddy black water ripple up and around my shins. It was cold and not at all what I was expecting.

Hartless waded through the water as fast as his legs could carry him and stood in front of me panting and looking very sorry for himself.

"When did they turn this place into an indoor pool?" I mumbled.

"I'm sorry, I t-t-tried to warn you, but it was too late."

"Funny how it's always too late around here, isn't it, Hartless!"

We made our way back out into the lobby. Hartless watched intently as I kicked off my shoes and threw my socks into a corner. He pushed up the brim of his hat with a finger.

"So, did you want to speak to me, Mr Mahoney?"

"No, I was looking for tickets to see the Grumbleweeds."

Hartless frowned before realising I was only joking. Even then he didn't laugh. He just watched me get to my feet and slip on my shoes. It was like stepping into two wet haddocks.

"So what can I do for you?"

He was nervous and it made me feel better. "I take it you know Frank Hebden?"

"Er, yes."

"How well?"

"Well I've interviewed him a couple of times."

"Interviewed, or stuck a mike in his face as he passed close by?"

Hartless was cross. "I know him, all right. I even like him. He's one of the few people who actually cares about this godforsaken t-town."

"So, what if I said I thought Hebden was having an affair with Helen Fitzsimmons?"

For a moment Hartless just looked at me. It was as if he was waiting for the punchline. Then he realised he'd already heard it and started to laugh.

I grabbed him by the collar and shoved him against the wall, hard.

"I'll let you know when I'm joking, Hartless!" I hissed.

He stopped laughing.

I stepped back and let him straighten his collar and tie.

"I'm s-s-sorry, Mr Mahoney, but if you knew Hebden you'd realise he's really not the kind to have an affair."

"Well I don't, that's why I'm asking you."

"Yes, I'm sorry. I realise th-th-that now."

"So what's Hebden got against women?"

"It's nothing t-t-to do with women, it's simply that he never gets the t-t-time. Believe me, the man's a workaholic. If there were eight days in the week he'd be there at his desk on the ninth!"

"So how come I found him polishing his boat the other day?"

Hartless pushed the rim of his hat a bit further back and took a short walk.

"Last year I arranged a special interview with Hebden, it was his t-t-tenth year in the job. I thought it would be interesting t-t-to see what he'd achieved. He invited me round to his house, laid on some food and drink, the works. We got on fine. And then, halfway through the evening and, much t-t-to my surprise, he told me something 'strictly off the record'."

"I'm listening."

"He t-t-told me that when he'd got the job he'd had big plans for the town. He felt it had so much potential. I remember him saying so at the time . . ."

"Yeah, he told me much the same thing this morning," I interrupted.

"Yes, well, all he's done since is plan roundabouts and traffic lights. Everything else, all his other ideas, are squashed because they aren't considered viable."

"What do you mean, viable?"

"He's always trying to balance public demand with the big businesses, people who just want to monopolise the trade here."

"People like Roger Laughton?"

Hartless nodded. "Hebden felt that he couldn't do anything right. Then, a couple of years ago there was all this trouble over the Valley Bridge."

"The one that everyone jumps off?"

Hartless nodded again. "It was getting a lot of bad publicity. I mean, there were people driving from all over the country just to commit suicide here."

"What's that got to do with Hebden?"

"People wanted something done about the bridge. To make it safe. But to Hebden it was a Victorian masterpiece, one of the focal points of the t-t-town. He worked day and night to find a solution. Unfortunately, he worked so hard he collapsed. Everybody thought he'd had a heart attack, but it was s-s-stress. He spent a week in hospital and that was all the time they needed to go ahead and fence off the bridge."

"He must have been gutted!"

"He moaned about how they'd turned a Victorian masterpiece into a giant cheesegrater. Anyway he was forced into finding a hobby, s-s-something to keep him away from work at least one day a week. That's why he has his father's boat."

Suddenly Hartless paused to chew on a thought.

"What?"

"It's probably nothing . . ."

"What's probably nothing?"

"Well, now you come to mention it, Hebden has changed a little, I mean, I'm sure he still cares about the town, but it's just that there's something different about him, that's all."

"Such as?"

"Well he isn't as enthusiastic as he used to be."

"That's hardly surprising though, is it? People can only take so many kicks before they stay down."

"Yes, I'm sure you're right. That must be it. But what made you think he was having an affair with Fitzsimmons?"

"She's convinced her ex is blackmailing her. She figured he was trying to muscle in on her old man's business. I haven't seen a lot of Colin Fitzsimmons, but if ever a man never wanted to be anybody it's him." I was looking at Hartless as I spoke and he was doing that thing with his mouth again.

"Surely everybody wants to be somebody . . ."

"Not him. He's stuck in the seventies with his plastic records and Star Wars videos."

Hartless looked at me. "You're not telling me everything, are you, Mr Mahoney?"

I glanced at him and then at nothing in particular. "I found some negatives next to the dead girl's body."

"Negatives, of what?"

"I don't know, I couldn't make them out."

Suddenly Hartless became anxious. "Have you s-s-still got them?"

I nodded.

"There's a man I know, that Ronnie used to see. He has a sh-sh-shop just round the corner from the office. He works wonders and never asks questions. You could try him, if you wanted."

I looked at Hartless, he was getting all excited again. It was time to leave.

"This could be just the break we've been waiting for, Mr Mahoney!"

"Yeah, and then again they might be pictures of Great Aunt Maud stuffing her face with candy floss. Then how are you going to feel?"

"But . . ."

"But nothing, Hartless. Like Walker said, nothing matters an ounce until we've got the facts. Then I'll start doing cartwheels."

"So, what are you going to do? If you don't mind me asking?"

"Take these negs to the shop and have a bath. All this raking around in the dirt and filth has finally taken its toll . . ."

~

The sign on the door said 'OPEN'. I turned the handle and pushed. The door moved three inches then stopped, a length of chain holding it tight.

I tapped on the glass and a figure appeared from behind the counter. An old man limped across the floor and shot me a lingering stare before unhooking the chain and pulling back the door without a word. A bell rang above me.

"I thought you were closed."

"I was having lunch," he said, waving a sandwich the size of a brick in my face.

He closed the door behind me and limped back to the counter at a pace slightly quicker than treacle. He was short and thin, with a bony face and bony hands. He had thick black hair greying at the temples. It was combed across his head with grease. The stubble on his chin was like sandpaper. He wore a baggy green cardigan, with low, bulging pockets.

I watched him crouch behind the counter and reappear with a flask covered in grease and tea stains. He held up a cup. I shook my head and watched as he poured tea into a small china cup. His hands shook, but he didn't spill a drop.

"What can I do for you?" he asked, adjusting the thick-rimmed glasses that doubled the size of his eyes whenever he looked at me.

I passed him the negatives. "Ronnie asked me to bring these over."

"Ronnie?"

"Yeah, Ronnie Elliott. The Private Investigator."

"Oh, of course, Ronnie. How is he?"

"He's been better," I hedged. What else could I say? I didn't want a little thing like Ronnie's untimely demise to ruin the old man's lunch.

He took another bite of the sandwich, wiped his hands down the sides of his trousers and pinched the negs between his fingers. His hands stopped shaking.

"They're not very good," I said.

He glanced at me with an expression that wouldn't have looked out of place in a morgue. Then he flicked a switch, lighting up the glass counter. He pressed the negatives against the glass and peered at them through a magnifying glass.

"Mmm," he mused. "Underexposed. Badly underexposed. Not enough light."

"Yeah, well I'm no David Bailey."

"You need to use a slower shutter speed."

"Like I said, I'm no David Bailey."

"They're black and white."

"Is that a problem?"

"They might be a little grainy. I'll have to use some special filters."

"Whatever it takes."

He stood up and took hold of his cup. His hand was shaking again.

"Come back on Thursday. After lunch. I'll have them ready for you then."

"Fine. Do I pay you now?"

He shook his head.

"Don't you need my name?"

"What difference will that make? Anyway, Ronnie sent you, didn't he?"

"Of course," I nodded. I found I was smiling as I stepped back into the daylight. I liked the old guy. I liked his manner. It was abrupt, but honest. I couldn't help thinking that if there were more people like him in the world, PIs would soon go out of business.

~

With nothing else to do, I went back to the guest house. I was tired and hungry. Barbara cooked me dinner and it was the first decent meal I'd had in days. Then I took a bath. It was Wednesday night and most of the residents were out praying to the Mecca god of numbers.

I filled the tub until it almost overflowed and lay there, happy in the

103

knowledge that I wasn't going to be disturbed by anyone banging on the door asking if they'd left their teeth in a jar by the sink.

The water was soothing, it eased my aching limbs and allowed my mind to escape from the reality of pretending to being a PI, and to concentrate on the illusion of trying to be an author. I was a legend in my own bathtub and revelled in the idea of being Tony Blake, author of the million seller, 'The Drowning Man', the book widely tipped to become Hollywood's next blockbuster thriller. I imagined how I'd be the topic of conversation on one of the late-night review shows; the 'panel' including a failed writer and part-time journalist, and the obligatory token female, representing a generation of readers unable to make up their own minds about the worth of literature. Their mission: to guard against the evil elements of sexism, racism and any other 'ism' that threaten to corrupt a world gone PC mad. They discuss my work in the same breath as Doyle and Hammett, and suggest that I might be the next Raymond Chandler. Their conversation hails my cutting wit, ear for dialogue and the way I spill just enough of the plot in each chapter to keep the reader guessing. They like that my hero is a romantic, a daydreamer, a pleasant release from the archetypal macho detectives on show elsewhere. They applaud how the women are seen as strong characters, the ones weaving webs of deceit to trap the gullible males.

Then, out of the blue, the daydream turns sour as the jaundiced failed author reflects on what he considers to be the weakness of the plot and how it all provides the writer with an excuse to dish out typical northern working-class humour. He feels the plot is simply an attempt to force the reader to sympathise with the central character who is not meant to have ideas above his social standing, and who is pushed from pillar to post. He goes on to argue that the novel is so sentimental as to be positively dripping with crocodile tears and no wonder Hollywood wants to buy it . . .

The water turned cold as the failed author cynically berated my novel. He's cool, calculating and finally convinces everyone else by suggesting that, whilst it was supposed to be a thriller, nothing ever actually happens.

I wait for one of the other panellists to retaliate, but they fail to respond. In my mind's eye they turn to look at me but have nothing to say.

I towelled myself down and put on some fresh clothes.

I needed to think things through, and walking seemed the best way to focus my mind. I made a right outside the B&B and walked along the cliff top. The sound of waves whooshing against the beach and breaking on the rocks below broke through the evening darkness. The street was still and lined with guest houses bravely braced against the northerly winds.

Most had large 'VACANCY' signs in the windows.

Dusk had fallen early, bringing with it a thick swirling fog that slipped down over the rooftops and wrapped itself around the ruined castle's high stone walls. A castle with no dungeons or secret passages, just freshly mown lawns and 'Keep Off' signs on the crumbling walls. A castle with no light to illuminate its place in history.

I like fog. I have always been fascinated by it. It doesn't fall like snow, or pour like rain or blaze like the sun. It creeps, glistens, clings and conceals footsteps that follow you somewhere in the distance. And though I tried hard to concentrate on Walker, Mandy and Hartless my ears strained to hear footsteps close behind. I couldn't turn around, because that would be too obvious, but nor did I want to quicken my pace either because that would suggest I was scared. But I was scared.

I took a left turn. It was a wrong turn. The road narrowed and came to a dead end several yards further on. I was faced with a brick wall, its top decorated with broken glass and barbed wire.

The footsteps closed in behind me.

I turned to see two figures emerge from the greyness. The same figures who'd stepped into Ronnie Elliott's office a few days ago.

"Of all the dead-ends, in all the alleyways, in all the world, you had to pick mine . . ." It was all I could come up with.

Short Suit inched a smile. "Always the comedian, eh, Mahoney."

"I find it helps get me through the day."

I watched his face light up in the flare of a match as he lit a cigarette.

"I suppose you want to know why I'm still working for Helen Fitzsimmons?"

He blew a smoke ring and shook his head. "Actually we haven't got time for polite conversation . . ."

Which was probably as well because he might have needed somebody to dictate it for him.

"What I'm looking for is some information."

"You mean like train times? Weather reports? That kind of thing?"

Short Suit was losing patience, but I was too busy staring at the gorilla taking heavy steps towards me to take much notice. I backed up against the wall. There was nowhere to run.

"This is Nails," said Short Suit. "You know why we call him 'Nails'?"

"Because he does a nice manicure?"

Short Suit took another drag and ran the tip of his finger down his scar.

"Because he enjoys hammering home a point."

"And what is the point, exactly?"

By now Nails was towering over me. He had lips the size of rubber tyres, a nose squashed deep into his face and eyebrows that wrapped themselves around one another in a line across his face. My mother had always told me that knitted eyebrows were a sign of madness and, right now, I couldn't find a single reason to doubt her.

"Where are the negatives, Mahoney?"

"Negatives?" I asked.

"Yeah. The negatives."

"And suppose I don't know what you're talking about?"

"Then this is going to hurt you far more than it hurts me."

I didn't get time to ask what. There was a short sharp pain across my cheek and I felt myself spinning towards the floor. A lonely star smiled at me through the fog. I could see the broken glass on top of the wall. I could see Nails massaging his knuckles. And then I could see no more.

~

The first thing I felt was pain, a cold, jarring pain like someone was squeezing the side of my face into a vice.

The first thing I heard was laughter, then the sound of a match as it struck the heel of a shoe and fizzed up through the air.

I came round sitting in a chair with my chin on my chest. The only thing stopping me from toppling forward onto the floor was the rope tied around my wrists behind the chair. It felt like I'd been sitting for hours. My neck ached, my shoulders ached, my face ached. I lifted my eyes and saw Short Suit behind a cloud of cigarette smoke a few feet in front of me. He had his right hand tucked into his coat pocket as if he had a concealed weapon and was pointing it at me. He pulled the cigarette from his mouth and wrapped his lips around a thin smile.

"Nice of you to join us again, Mahoney."

I was about to crack a line when the side of my face exploded with pain and I remembered the fog, the dead end and Nails throwing his fist at me.

Short Suit stepped forward and waved his cigarette in my face.

"You don't look so good, Mahoney!"

I gritted my teeth and muttered, "But I still look a whole lot better than you!"

He laughed, a pleasant, 'butter wouldn't melt in his mouth', kind of laugh.

"Sorry about Nails," he said. "He just doesn't know his own strength."

I tried to ease the pain in my body by moving about, but Nails dropped a paw the size of a manhole cover onto my shoulder and held me still.

"So this is how it is, Mahoney," said Short Suit, running a finger up and down his scar. "You answer our questions and we let you go. We can't be any more reasonable than that now, can we?"

"Like I said before, I don't know what you're talking about."

I should have known what was going to happen next. I was practically asking for it after all. But I didn't even get time to flinch. There was a crack across the side of my face and I swear I was struck by lightning. I ended up on the floor in a big ugly heap. My shoulder took most of the impact, and at least that took some of the pain away from my face.

Nails lifted me like a cushion and dumped me back into a seated position while the room spun and the dust settled.

The beating was slowly bringing me to my senses, my sense of fear in particular. I began to realise that, amongst all the questions and blind alleys and goose chases only one thing was certain, death. It didn't matter what you did or what you said, death just sat there patiently waiting with a smug, self-satisfied smile knowing that sooner or later you'd slip into his open arms.

But it was one thing knowing I was going to die, and quite another knowing how. I was alone in a room with two men who made a living out of killing people. And they were probably very good at it. They'd quite happily strap concrete boots to my feet and dump me in the sea and think as much about that as ordering their lunch. Their livelihood might be the death of me.

But if I was going to die, I wanted it to be quick. I wanted to be sitting there one minute and floating on a cloud plucking a harp the next, with nothing in between, especially the no pain bit. But mostly I wanted to live, and the trouble with that was it meant giving them what they wanted. And even then, I couldn't be sure of walking out alive.

I had to stall and piece together what was going on.

Short Suit cupped my chin in his right hand and offered me a pitiful tut.

"All right, Mahoney, let's try this one more time. Give us the negatives!"

"What makes you so sure I have them?"

"We saw you take them."

"When?"

"When you found Fitzsimmons and the girl."

They had been following me. All the time. Watching my every move. Who were these guys?

"I gave them to the police."

Short Suit sucked on his cigarette and sniggered as he blew smoke into my face. "Don't lie to me!"

"What makes you so sure I am?"

Although I was half expecting it, it didn't help. We went through the whole damn routine; crack, pain, fall, pain, lift, pain.

"This is a life or death situation, Mahoney. You give me the negatives and you live. You don't, and . . . well you know the rest."

There was a lump the size of a football rising up from where my nose had been and the room was fast fading from view. I choked on a mouthful of blood and spat it out, missing a pair of shiny brogues by inches.

"So what's in it for me?" I croaked.

Short Suit glanced down at the blood, then across at me and laughed like it was the funniest thing he'd ever heard. "I like you, Mahoney," he said, waving a finger at me. "You've got balls."

Then he stopped smiling.

"What makes you think there's anything in this for you, other than we don't break your neck?"

"The fact that I know where the negatives are and you don't. Sure, you can bang me around, but that's just going to waste a lot of time, when all you have to do is give me what I want."

"And that is?"

"Five grand."

"Five grand!"

I watched his eyebrows do little bunny hops across his face while his smile grew wider by the second. Pretty soon he was going to need an extra set of teeth. "You're joking, right!"

"Think about it. If they're worth killing for, they must be worth at least that much, probably more . . ."

Suddenly his eyes narrowed and he stopped smiling. The fact that I wasn't reading from the same script made him start to sweat. He dropped onto a crate and did that thing with his face again, running the tip of a finger up and down the length of the scar as if he hoped it would go away. He glanced at Nails, but sensed that asking him to consider anything other than breaking bones would have reduced him to ash.

Time slipped by . . .

"All right," he said, eventually. "You've got a deal. You get the negatives and I'll get you your money." He stood up and waved the cigarette at me again. "We'll meet here tomorrow at six."

"Yeah, and maybe you'd like me to bring my own gun and shoot myself when we're finished, just to save you the trouble!"

"I don't understand."

"It's simple. There's no way I'm meeting the two of you here alone!"
"What's the matter, Mahoney, don't you trust me?" he sounded hurt.
"Like I'd trust a three-legged donkey to win the National."
"So what then?"
"We'll meet the day after tomorrow."
"Why so long?"
"Because I said so!"
"Time and place?"
"Seven, at the Harbour Cafe on the foreshore."
"Why?"
"Because it sells nice ice-cream!"
"You're smart, Mahoney. And that bothers me. So here's a little reminder just in case you think about getting any fancy ideas."

Nails moved in and the lights went out again . . .

15

I looked in the mirror. It's something I don't do very often. I don't like what I see. All those childhood dreams wrapped up in the memory of a thirty-six-year-old nobody can be hard to live with at times. I wiped away the condensation and peered into the reflection of someone with a face like a bashed crab. My left eye was virtually shut and my left cheek glowed like a beacon. I dabbed the bruises carefully with a cold flannel. Not that it mattered how careful I was, it still hurt like hell.

After making myself a coffee and picking some ice cubes from the freezer, I went up to my room, switched on the TV and stretched out on the bed. I lay there for a while, happy in the luxury of being one of life's spongers, the proverbial couch potato, it allowed me the freedom to let someone else do all the thinking and all the doing. I hoped watching some mindless sitcom would free my mind from all its unanswered questions.

There was a black and white movie on. At least I thought it was black and white, but it was hard to tell considering I didn't have a colour set. It starred Cagney and Bogart. I'd seen it before and loved it, but I couldn't recall the title. Bogart and Cagney have known each other from the war and have gone into business together. But things get out of hand, and Cagney shoots Bogart. Bogart has just enough breath to fire back. Cagney takes it like a man and staggers to the cathedral steps where he falls dead in the snow. The love of his life weeps over his shoulder while this big 'Crime doesn't pay' message flashes across the screen like we're really supposed to believe it.

Unfortunately I wanted them both to survive. I wanted them to beat the system and live to fight another day. They were my heroes, I'd grown up with characters such as Bogart and Cagney, Price and Lee, the bad guys, the ones people always remembered. And it made me wonder, who on earth would ever remember me?

As the credits rolled I thought back to Short Suit and Nails. They wanted me dead. All that was keeping me alive was the negatives.

The police wanted me locked up. All that was keeping me out of jail was circumstance.

There had to be something else, something Helen Fitzsimmons wasn't telling me. It was time she knew I was through with being taken for a ride. I had to get tough. Bogart wouldn't have been messed around like I was. He always got what he wanted. If I wanted answers I had to become more like him and go out and get them.

~

Helen Fitzsimmons stood in the library pouring brandy. She was wearing an expensive necklace over an expensive blouse with an even more expensive gloat on her face. She held up a glass.

"Bourbon on the rocks," I said as I tugged on my ear.

She raised an eyebrow at me like she was impressed. Not that I cared. I mean, if she hadn't been. I wasn't suddenly going to ask for a lemonade.

I watched the bourbon spin round the edge of the glass and down around the ice. She handed me the glass and perched herself on a barstool. I watched as she crossed her legs ever so purposefully. Most of her right thigh looked up at me as if asking what I was waiting for.

"So tell me, Mr Mahoney, did you come all this way just to look at my legs or have you got something else in mind?"

"Unfortunately I have."

"And what might that be I wonder, Mr Big Private Investigator?"

"Your brother."

"What about him?"

"That's what I'd like to know." I was staring down into my glass, trying to block her legs from my mind.

"I'm not sure I know what to tell you."

"Anything."

"Such as?"

"How he came to die in six inches of water?" I had to admit it wasn't

110

the most subtle question I'd ever asked, but I was tired and hungry for answers and it forced Helen Fitzsimmons from her pedestal. She paused to sip her drink and then looked across the room as if searching for a distant memory.

"It was a horrible accident. Our boat capsized. Eric was knocked unconscious. I was carried downstream. Someone found his body face down in the water just a yard from the riverbank . . ."

Her voice was soft, her eyes glistened, and for a moment I felt sorry for having asked. But only for a moment.

"So how come the press made such a big deal out of it?"

"Isn't that their job?"

"Maybe, but then again, there's no smoke without fire . . ."

She looked at me, smiled, slipped off the stool and walked towards me like she had the first time I met her at the restaurant, hips swaying, heels tapping. She stopped just short of my nose and ran a finger along the side of my face, the side that had since turned purple.

"That looks extremely painful."

Her touch was soft and gentle and just what I needed. The trouble was I didn't need it right now.

She reached across to kiss me on the other cheek. Her lips were soft and moist. Her perfume strong. It was nicer than having Nails beat me to a pulp, but it bothered me.

So I sipped my bourbon and didn't say a word. When she tried it again I took hold of her wrist and held it tight. She looked at me as if she ached to slap my face.

"What's the matter, Mr Private Investigator, scared a little affection might lower your guard? Or is it all part of being the big tough detective?"

"I don't know. You'll have to ask a big tough detective."

I let go of her and she propped herself up against the bar.

"I have a theory," I said.

"Oh, go ahead, I do love a good story."

"Your old man is nearing retirement, you see the chance to move in on some action, but you're worried that he's too old-fashioned to even consider you, so . . ."

"What! I kill my own brother!"

I had to admit it did sound far-fetched hearing the words said aloud.

"Is that what you're suggesting, Mr Mahoney?"

"Like I said, it's only a theory . . ."

"And what about Colin? I suppose I disposed of him as well?"

I stood with the empty glass in my hand and listened to her laugh.

Somehow I'd got backed into a corner by a very clever lady.

"But if that were true, then why did I hire you to follow him?"

"Well, that's the beauty of it. I'm just a low-life PI who happened to get his fingerprints all over Colin's apartment and I haven't got a single good reason for being there. You've got me right where you want me."

She was intrigued. "Not quite," she smiled and started towards me again. When she was close enough she whispered, "I know what your game is, Mr Private Investigator."

"You do?" my voice was scarcely more than a whisper.

She wobbled on a heel. I caught her arm and held her close.

"You see a rich, powerful and vulnerable woman and you think . . ." she crushed her lips to mine, her tongue searching my mouth as a hand massaged the back of my neck drawing me closer still, ". . . that you can take advantage of her!"

She kissed me again.

"And there's me thinking that's what you wanted!"

Her eyes grew large as she stamped her foot and waved an arm towards the door. Most of her drink flew out over the floor. But she either didn't notice, or she didn't care.

"I think you should leave, right now!"

"Why? Because I speak my mind? And there's me thinking you liked Private Investigators who didn't care about the size of their wallets."

"Right this minute!" Helen Fitzsimmons slammed her drink onto the bar and headed for the phone as fast as her dress would allow. "I'm going to call . . ."

I moved to her side and caught hold of her hand, preventing her from dialling. "I didn't think you wanted the police involved!"

She turned and slapped my face. In view of what I'd been through over the past twenty-four hours it hurt like hell. It also made me angry and it must have showed because she suddenly recoiled as if she thought I was going to strike her.

"You wouldn't hit a lady, would you?"

"Maybe not. But what's that got to do with you?"

She rolled her eyes to the ceiling and did her best not to fall over. She staggered back to the bar to pour herself another drink.

"So what are you going to do now, Mr Big Detective, beat me till I confess?"

It was a thought but I had the strangest feeling she'd probably enjoy it.

"Why not just give me a straight answer?"

"Such as what I might gain from all these deaths, I suppose?"

"Something like that."

"Absolutely nothing!"

"Nothing? What about your old man's business?"

Helen Fitzsimmons let out a laugh. "My old man's business, as you so nicely put it . . . Do you know anything about my old man's business?"

"Only that it eats up half of Scarborough."

"And that makes him what? Rich, powerful, loved?"

"It makes him something."

"Well maybe it did once, when this pathetic little town was actually worth something, when people came from all over the country and stayed for more than just a weekend and spent every last penny they had. But that was a long time ago . . ." She sounded wistful.

"Meaning?"

"Meaning my father isn't worth a penny now."

I found that hard to believe. "What about the restaurants and hotels?"

"Two restaurants, one hotel. That's all he has left. The restaurants make just about enough to stay afloat and the hotel collapsed into the sea a short while ago."

"That was his?"

She nodded. "Well, it was my brother's actually. Unfortunately it hadn't made a penny in years, which is why the press assumed he'd been killed for the insurance. It had never crossed my mind." She took a moment to gather her thoughts and left her drink on the bar. "After the accident father put all he had left into refurbishing the hotel. I think he felt guilty. They were never close. But six months later it collapsed without a helping hand from anyone. Funny, isn't it? You do what you can for the town and it just turns its back on you when things get tough."

"But if all that's true, why would Colin try to blackmail him?"

She slumped into a chair without bothering to remove the dust sheet. "Now you come to mention it, I really have no idea."

I looked at Helen Fitzsimmons and for the first time since I'd met her I felt she was telling me the truth. I poured myself another drink. Not that it helped, the questions continued to swirl blindly around my head.

"Do you really believe I'm capable of murder, Mr Mahoney?"

"To be honest I hadn't given it much thought. I'm too busy knowing too much about what I shouldn't know and not enough about what I should." I slipped on my coat. "But if it's not your old man's money they're after then it's got to be something or somebody else."

Helen Fitzsimmons got to her feet. She looked frightened. "I wish you hadn't said that!"

"I'm not too thrilled about it either."

She held my arm and squeezed it tight. "Do you have to leave?"

"I'm not going to find any answers here . . . not the answers I'm looking for anyway." I tried to pull away but she held me tight. I looked into her eyes and kissed her.

"I'm scared," she whispered.

So was I, but I couldn't bring myself to admit it to her.

16

It wasn't often I'd had the pleasure of sleeping in my bed at the guest house, but when I had I'd woken to the sun slipping in through a chink in the curtains and the shrill of gulls the size of eagles perched on the window ledge impersonating the three tenors. Unfortunately this particular morning was different. This particular morning a fist was beating the hell out of my door. I crossed the room and opened it before someone smashed their knuckles.

It was Walker.

"What the hell have you got against my door?"

"It reminds me of you!" he said, inviting himself in.

I closed the door and studied it closely. "You mean tall and tough?"

"I mean, it keeps getting in my way!"

Walker had his hands in his jacket pockets and was pacing the floor. The jacket was creased and the five o'clock shadow across his chin was showing 8.15.

He caught sight of my face. "What the hell happened to you?"

"I upset a couple of locals."

"Now why doesn't that surprise me!"

"You could try taking my side."

"Are they still alive?"

"They were when they left me."

"Well that's a start I suppose. So what did they want?"

"I don't know. They didn't say. People like that don't usually need a reason, do they?"

Walker shrugged and continued pacing the floor. I was worried he'd wear a hole in the carpet and I'd be left with the bill.

"Where were you last night, Mahoney?"

"When last night?"

"When you weren't getting yourself beaten up."

"Here."

"All night?"

I didn't answer.

"All night?"

I paused for a second, but it was enough for Walker. He pinned me to the wall. He didn't look happy.

"All night?"

"Yeah, well apart from when I went to see Helen Fitzsimmons."

"And what did you go there for?"

"Is that any of your business?"

"I'm making it my business!"

We were face to face, eyeball to eyeball, like two drunks in a bar-room brawl. But I'd already had one kicking too many and I wasn't in the mood for another.

"I wanted to know why she lied to me."

"About what?"

"About why she wanted me to follow Colin Fitzsimmons."

"And then what?"

"I came back here."

"What time was that?"

"Christ, Walker, you're worse than my mother!"

He pressed me harder against the wall. "What time?"

"I don't know, eleven, eleven-thirty. I had a drink, then went to bed."

Walker let go of me and stepped back. I was relieved, I mean, who the hell are you supposed to turn to when the cops start beating you up?

"Mind telling me what all this is about?"

The Inspector was at the window. On a clear day you could see right across the street to all the other guest houses. But today it was foggy.

"How was Helen Fitzsimmons when you left her?"

"One sip short of a ready-made hangover. Why?"

Walker turned his back to the window and let out a heavy sigh. "Her body was found early this morning."

I looked back at Walker and convinced myself that I'd never heard the word 'dead' so often in such a short space of time.

I sat on the bed and thought about Helen Fitzsimmons and her legs looking up at me. How only last night her tongue had been searching my mouth, and me thinking that she'd just killed two people.

"How?" I asked.

"It looks like suicide . . ."

"Another suicide! Christ! I thought sea air was supposed to be good for you!"

"I said it looks like, Mahoney. I didn't say it was."

"Don't tell me you're beginning to believe that something is going on after all?"

Walker slumped into a chair and rubbed his eyes.

"I'm not sure what to think any more."

Walker needed inspiration. I wanted to throw him an 'I told you so' line but I didn't know what to say exactly.

"And I suppose that by coming round here you think I've got something to do with whatever it is you think might have happened?"

He looked at me and then at the floor. "I've just been speaking to Roger Laughton. He told me about the money his daughter paid you."

"That's right."

"Apparently you were complaining it was too much?"

"So?"

"Isn't that a bit unusual?"

"What, that you've found somebody with a conscience?"

"There are people, Mahoney, people in high places, who think you might have been blackmailing Helen Fitzsimmons."

"People like you, or idiots like Superintendent Matthews?"

"So were you? Blackmailing Helen Fitzsimmons?"

"And what the hell would I have on her?"

Walker stood up impatiently. He looked desperate for a drink. But instead of insisting on a beer he poked a finger at me.

"You think you're smart don't you, Mahoney?"

"I'm only smart because you ask so many dumb questions."

We stared each other out.

Eventually I said, "You're clutching at straws, Walker. If you really had something on me you'd have arrested me by now."

He looked at me and yawned. He was tired and ready to go back to his happy home and his happy family with their smiling faces and solid brick walls.

"I take it that means you don't think I'm guilty?"

"It's not that," he said, shaking his head. "I just can't be bothered with all the paperwork!"

He had an incredibly reassuring way with words.

"If you're guilty, you'll slip up and I'll be ready and waiting when you do."

I looked at Walker. It was hard to distinguish him from the two bozos whose fists I'd run into the previous night. I followed him to the door. It took me that long to decide to tell him about Hartless.

"I ran into a guy called Eddie Hartless yesterday," I offered.

"I know that name."

"He's a journalist."

"Went to the right person if he was looking for a story then, didn't he!"

I ignored the smirk on Walker's face.

"He wanted to know why the police were covering up Ronnie Elliott's death."

Walker stopped smirking. "So what did you tell him?"

"So do I."

"Get to the point, Mahoney!"

"He said that Ronnie was due to meet someone the night he died."

"Who?"

"He didn't know."

Walker let out an impatient sigh and reached for the door.

"But he thinks he might be able to find out who it was, if you're interested that is."

"Right," said Walker, prodding a finger into my chest, "the moment he does, you give me a call, you hear me, Mahoney? From now on I want to know where you are every minute of every day. Do I make myself clear?"

"If I didn't know any better, Walker, I'd think you cared!"

"And if I didn't know you any better, I probably would!"

~

Walker's presence had caused a stir among the guest house's other residents. Edith mentioned she'd never seen anything so exciting in the twenty-two years she'd been coming to Scarborough, while Maude wasn't convinced Walker was a policeman at all, on account of his creased clothes and unkempt appearance.

"It's no wonder nobody respects the law any more, you can't tell the difference between them and the villains!" she kept repeating to no one in particular.

Reg just hoped all the early morning activity wouldn't delay his bacon and eggs.

I wasn't in the mood for breakfast. All the corpses had taken care of that. Last night I'd practically accused Helen Fitzsimmons of killing her brother and her husband. How sad was that? How wrong could I be?

I needed something, anything. I needed those photos.

I headed straight for the shop where I'd dropped off the negatives. Or as close as I could get because a police car was blocking the entrance to the street. I parked up, got out and walked the rest of the way.

A large crowd had gathered on the pavement. A policeman stood in front of them, watching as they looked and pointed above and beyond a parked fire engine.

A man in a heavy black jacket and bright yellow helmet ushered me onto the pavement and into the crowd. From there I could see the shop. Or what remained of it. The red brick walls were covered with thick black soot. The large plate-glass window was scattered in a thousand pieces on the road. The shop looked like a cave; a dark, damp, gloomy cave with raindrops dripping from the ceiling and circles of smoke twisting up into what was left of a bright blue morning.

The old man was standing across the street talking to a woman in a uniform. He looked like he'd lost everything on a horse that was still to come in. He was screwing a finger deep into his ear and looking puzzled and confused.

I stood in front of the crowd and listened to the rumours circulate. They touched on everything, from delinquents roaming the town and causing mayhem, to an insurance scam and how the owner would never get away with it.

Eventually the woman in uniform put away her notebook and left the owner alone. He perched on the bumper of one of the fire engines, his head in his hands. I called out to him, but he didn't recognise me at first.

"You're Ronnie's friend!"

I nodded. "Are you all right?"

He got to his feet, stuck his hands deep inside the bottomless pockets of his cardigan and made his way towards me.

"Apart from being woken up at six in the morning to find that my shop's been burnt to a cinder, then yes, I suppose I am."

It was a daft question.

"Look, I hope you don't mind me asking, but the negs I dropped off the other day, the ones you said weren't very good . . ."

"Aye," he replied, gazing back at the shop. "Well they're even worse now. Twenty-five years I put into this place. Twenty-five years and every last penny gone up in smoke just like that." He snapped his thumb and middle finger together.

"But you're insured, right?"

"Insured?" He laughed. "For what it's worth I'm insured. But they'll hardly come rushing to me with a cheque, will they? Besides, what's anybody going to give me for a pile of old cameras?"

"You lost everything?"

He put a finger in his ear and nodded.

For a moment we just stood and stared at the ruins, both of us asking, why me? Why now?

"Any idea how it started?" I asked.

"Somebody said they saw two men hanging around late last night. But it's like it always is, once the police get involved, folk seem to forget everything but their own name."

"Yeah, well, I'm sorry all the same."

The old man limped back to the shop leaving me to reflect on yet another lost opportunity. Fate had again lifted me from my knees and dropped me onto my backside. If there was a light at the end of the tunnel it was nothing more than a speeding train . . .

Without the prints I had nothing. Not only was I unable to prove that something was going on, but who knew what Short Suit and Nails had in store for me when they finally caught up with me again?

I had one last throw of the dice. Roger Laughton. If somebody was trying to blackmail him then they had to have a pretty good reason. Doubtless Laughton had trodden on a few toes in his time, all I had to do was find the feet they belonged to. Laughton had to come clean. His daughter was dead, that had to mean something, even if he was old-fashioned and sexist.

I drove up to his house but he wasn't at home. His wife told me I'd find him over in Peasholm Park. Apparently he went there when he needed time to himself.

At first I couldn't help thinking that a park would be the last place that I'd have looked for Laughton, there was just no way he could make any money from it. But then again, beyond the colourful flowers and neatly cut grass stood narrow walkways with overgrown bushes and muddy waters littered with traffic cones and shopping trolleys. This was Scarborough all over, neat and trim on the outside but a whole lot of dirt and waste on the inside. All in all it was the perfect place for Laughton to hang out.

The old man was resting on a bench, listening to a band playing on a floating platform in the middle of the park's lake. Rowing-boats shaped like giant swans passed close by. His legs were crossed and he massaged his forehead with a hand.

I stood for a moment, unsure of what to do next. The last time we'd met he'd said he'd hold me responsible if anything happened to his daughter. Now she was dead and he'd be feeling more hurt than I could imagine.

I couldn't be sure, but I had the feeling the pained expression on his face when he saw me was instinctive.

"Ah! Mr Private Investigator! Are you here to enjoy the band or to track down folk who don't return their boats on time?"

"Actually I wanted to say sorry about Helen."

Laughton forced a smile but had a hard time trying not to let his feelings show.

"The police said she committed suicide."

"Yes," said Laughton. "They told me the same thing."

"Doesn't that surprise you?"

"Nothing Helen does . . . did, surprised me." Laughton looked out across the lake and smiled. "She hated the water, but she used to make me bring her here every Sunday so she could learn to row, even if it meant going round and round in circles most of the time."

"She was trying to protect you!"

He appeared surprised. "Protect me! From what?"

"She thought someone was trying to blackmail you."

He started to cough and took out a handkerchief which he held to his mouth.

"Now if that's true," I continued, "what is it they've got on you?"

"Is that why Helen hired you?"

I nodded.

"But you still have no idea what's going on?"

"I can't help what people do and don't tell me!"

"So you wasted my daughter's time and her money and now you want to waste mine!"

"The trouble is you haven't got a whole lot of either left, have you?"

The old man looked at me. His face was red, the coughing had exhausted him.

"I don't know what you're talking about."

He got to his feet and started to make his way slowly around the lake, but I wasn't through with him yet. I took hold of his arm and held it tight.

"What bothers you most, Laughton? The possibility that somebody's got your number, or the fact that your daughter went to a complete stranger in her hour of need?"

For a second I thought he was going to punch me in the face. Instead he turned and walked away.

"Are you going to let your daughter die and never know the reason why?"

He kept on walking.

"You're dying, Laughton. Maybe you ought to think about doing one last good deed before you meet your maker."

He turned the corner and was gone.

~

I went back to the office. I don't know why. It just seemed as good a place as any.

I rinsed my face at the sink. The swelling around my eye had started to go down. I hoped I'd pushed Laughton far enough to make him come up with something, anything. The trouble was it had to be soon. I was running out of time. It was four o'clock. In a little over twenty-four hours Short Suit and Nails would come looking for me and the prints I hadn't got.

I looked out of the window and across the busy street. There were people everywhere, but I'd never felt more alone.

Out in the hall a narrow stretch of light peeked out from beneath Mandy Woodhall's door. I tapped on the glass and a voice invited me in. The room was much the same size as Ronnie's office, but the decor was more upmarket. There was a computer on the desk, a lamp with a neck like a giraffe, comfy leather chairs and the scent of someone a whole lot more appealing than Ronnie Elliott. There were a couple of wooden crates stacked with files, but Mandy was nowhere to be seen.

I walked up to the desk. "Mandy?"

"Won't be a minute," she called from a small room at the back of the office.

I picked up a photo standing on her desk. It was of Mandy with an elderly man and woman. They were on the beach. They looked happy.

Mandy stepped into the office. She looked how she always looked, a million dollars plus change.

"Your parents?" I asked, holding up the picture.

"Yes."

"You look really close."

She took the picture from me and studied it for a second. But only for a second. "We were."

"Were?" I asked, wondering if it was really any of my business.

"They're both dead!" She dropped the picture into one of the crates.

"I'm sorry."

"Why? It wasn't your fault!"

"Yeah I know, but I'm sorry all the same."

Mandy looked pale, drawn, tired and not at all the same girl I'd met in the bar a few days before. She sat at the desk.

"Hey, look, I'm sorry, I've caught you at a bad time, I . . ."

"No!" she said, waving a hand up at me. "It's me. I'm . . ."

She planted her elbows on the desk and let out a deep sigh. "I'm sick of all this." Her eyes skimmed across the room and I presumed she was talking about the crates.

"You're leaving?"

She nodded, and stood up again, unsettled.

"I was kind of hoping you were just untidy!"

A faint, very faint, smile pierced her lips. "Things aren't getting any better. I'm behind with the rent. I have to leave."

"And go where?"

"I don't know," she said. "Somewhere where I haven't upset anybody."

"You shouldn't worry about upsetting people. I do it all the time!"

"That's your job."

"Yeah, and I'm pretty good at it right now."

We were standing face to face. She was smiling again but I couldn't be sure what she was thinking.

"Look, I . . ." But the ringing of the telephone from Ronnie's office cut me short. I looked at Mandy. "I'd better go and see who that is."

She nodded and I cursed my way back to the office with the promise that, unless it was a close relative about to leave me all their worldly possessions, I would hang, draw and quarter them.

"Hello."

"Er . . . Mr Mahoney?"

"Yeah."

"Oh I'm . . . I'm glad I caught you."

"Who is this?"

"It's me, Eddie, Eddie Hartless."

I immediately pictured a noose tightening around his neck.

"I'm er, s-s-sorry to bother you, Mr Mahoney, but I was wondering if you were busy right now."

I looked back in the general direction of Mandy's office door and thought about the two of us waking up next to one another sometime tomorrow.

"Well, yeah, as a matter of fact . . ."

But Hartless was a journalist and taking no for an answer was something he was trained to ignore. "It's just that . . ."

"It's just that what?"

"Well I've, er, I've arranged t-t-to meet someone."

"Who?"

"I'd rather not discuss it over the phone, if it's all the same to you, Mr Mahoney. Suffice t-t-to say it's about Ronnie . . ."

Bugger! "When?"

"In about half an hour."

Bugger! Bugger!

"Where?"

"The lighthouse."

"This better be good, Hartless. In fact, this better be better than good."

Going back to Mandy after talking to Hartless was like having a seagull crap on my fish and chips. She was sat at her desk rummaging through the paperwork. Whatever moment there might have been had gone. Long gone. She looked up at me as I stood in the doorway.

"Was it something important?"

"Unfortunately, yes."

"A lead?"

"Eddie Hartless."

"The journalist?"

"Yeah, he reckons he might have something important."

"Did he say what?"

"No, he didn't want to speak over the phone. He wants me to meet him down at the lighthouse . . ."

Mandy stood up and walked towards me. "When?"

I checked my watch and wished the second hand wasn't moving so quickly.

"Now."

"You never know, it could be the break you're looking for."

"Are you still going to be here when I get back?" I asked.

"Probably not."

Bugger!

She kissed me like she had that first time in the office. Then she looked at me and smiled. "But, then again . . ."

~

Hartless had sounded nervous over the phone. Even more nervous than the last time we'd spoken. But then again Eddie Hartless probably got nervous every time he caught sight of his own reflection in the mirror.

I pulled up outside the amusement arcades on the foreshore and walked onto the pier. The night was cold. I warmed my hands into a fist and listened to the bellow of the foghorn and the gentle kiss of the waves against the moored boats.

It was five past seven. I was late and Hartless was nowhere to be seen.

The stagnant smell of fish rose up from the trawler nets and lobster pots littering the harbour walls. I hated fish and everything about the sea.

To get to the lighthouse I had to walk across the narrow footbridge that spanned both stretches of the pier. The wooden planks creaked and groaned with each step. The black sea lurked below, breathing in and breathing out against the harbour wall. I hurried to the other side.

Hiding in the shadow of the lighthouse a lonely figure huddled on a stool, his face buried deep into his hands, his eyes staring out through the mist to where a faint black line disappeared into the sea.

I'd never seen the point of fishing. Some people called it challenging. But I failed to see the challenge in sticking a worm on a hook and using it as bait to snare some poor unfortunate piece of sea-life.

The man was trying to light a cigarette.

"Nothing like a fresh sea breeze to make you feel alive, is there?"

Two narrow red eyes looked up at me through a gap in a large woolly hat and a wraparound scarf. He had a large purple nose and large purple cheeks.

Without saying a word he struck the match. This time he was successful. He dipped his face into the smoke and came up looking like a man possessed.

"Sod that," he mumbled. "I'd rather be at home in front of the fire with a pint of beer."

"So why aren't you?"

"You'd only ask a question like that if you'd never met the wife!"

I turned to see how serious he was, but he wasn't there any more. He was on his feet pulling hard on the line. The rod bent double and for about three seconds I was fascinated.

"What is it, do you a think, a bream?"

"Doubt it," he moaned.

"Too heavy?" I asked.

"Bloody lost more like! They're freshwater fish!"

He never took his eyes off the line, not even for a second, but there was a change in his voice. It was one of delight, the pride of a man overcoming nature.

I wanted to reach out and cut the line, but I didn't have to bother because as the fish rose up from the waters it snapped and the old man went two-stepping back across the pier. He came to a halt just short of the lighthouse.

Three cheers for mother nature.

"Sod that!" he growled. Coughing, he picked up the rod and walked back to the edge of the pier. His determined expression hadn't changed.

"Got away, did it?"

"For now," he winced.

I left him mumbling and set about finding Hartless.

There was a small packing factory at the end of the pier. A flicker of light and a low hum came from within. The large wooden door was slightly ajar. I heaved it open and stepped inside.

The room was only slightly colder than it was outside and the place stank of fish. A fluorescent light flickered high above like a dying flame. The humming sound was emanating from a large silver container at one end of the room. Every so often the lip of the container crashed open and sent a rush of fish onto the conveyor belt below. I followed the belt between a row of buckets that stood empty because the fish were piling up on the floor at the far end of the belt.

I was hypnotised by the fish, by the whites of their eyes. They were the kind of eyes that haunted my nightmares. They didn't blink and they showed no emotion. Dead or alive they just stared, deep into my innermost thoughts.

And in the flickering light, I caught sight of another pair of eyes that moved slowly along the belt. But these eyes were unlike the others. They were white and staring, but were filled with emotion, these eyes were full of pain.

I reached for the stop button. The belt came to a halt and I walked slowly to the eyes. They were buried under a school of fish that had learnt all they were ever going to know. The light buzzed and flickered for the last time. And in the darkness a hand reached out and touched my wrist.

"Shit!" I jumped back across the room and landed on the floor. From there I sat and followed the bright beam from the lighthouse as it travelled across the room, onto the belt and out into the darkness again. But nothing moved.

~

The police kept me waiting an hour. An hour alone in a room with just a desk, two chairs and the linger of cigarette smoke from a previous interrogation for company. At first I didn't mind, because I couldn't see the point. I hadn't committed a crime so I had nothing to worry about. But slowly the silence started to play with my imagination and I wound up thinking there was no need for bright lights and thumbscrews, just leave people alone with their thoughts long enough and eventually they'd admit to anything.

Most of the images inside my head were of Eddie Hartless lying dead on the conveyor belt. And what bothered me about those images was that, although I realised it was no way for anyone to die, I felt no sense of loss. I tried to convince myself that it was simply because all I knew about Hartless was that he was a journalist. But it wasn't that at all. Despite the fact that he was a journalist, and I don't like journalists, he was good at his job, not good enough for one of the big city papers perhaps, but good enough to work here on a second-rate local rag. And that bothered me. Because Eddie was good at his job, he could probably afford a nice flat with nice carpets while I had practically nothing in comparison. All I had was a rented bedsit. I lived on the dole. I was a mediocre writer with ambition, and an even worse PI.

I listened to the echo of my shoes as I paced the tiled floor and realised that not only was I was jealous but, worse still, I was jealous of a dead man.

~

Eventually the door opened and Sergeant O'Neal stepped inside, closely followed by Superintendent Matthews.

"Where's Walker?" I asked.

"Busy." O'Neal smirked as he pulled out a chair and sat down. He indicated he wanted me to do likewise.

I sat down and watched Matthews press his back against a wall and adjust his polka-dot bow tie.

"Tell me, Mr Mahoney, what were you doing down on the pier tonight?" O'Neal asked.

I had a smart answer. I had a lot of smart answers. I carried them around with me alongside the chip on my shoulder. They were my defence, my only defence. I wasn't big enough to stand up and hit someone and wasn't quick enough to run the other way when trouble came calling. So I tried to cut people down to size with words. But even though I detested O'Neal, it was clear I had to toe the line for the time being. I bit my lip. I had to be civil. I had to sit tight and pray that I would be dealt a better hand.

"I was supposed to be meeting Eddie Hartless."

"The journalist?"

"So he told me."

"What for?"

I paused and looked at Matthews.

"What for?" insisted O'Neal.

"He had this idea that Ronnie Elliott hadn't committed suicide. He rang me up and said he wanted to meet me."

"Why?"

"He said he had some important information."

"What kind of information?"

"He didn't say, he didn't want to talk over the phone."

"Why?"

"He was nervous."

"Of what?"

"Of all kinds of things."

"So you agreed to meet him?"

I nodded as Matthews struck a match. We both looked up as he lit a cigarette.

"And?" said O'Neal.

"Obviously somebody got to him before I did."

O'Neal let out a low sigh and stood up. He stretched his long limbs and walked around the room. All the while Matthews smoked his cigarette and didn't say a word.

"This is all very convenient, Mahoney."

There was something in the way O'Neal spoke, something that suggested he knew more than he was letting on, something I knew I was going to regret if I continued to play straight into his hands.

"What is?" I asked.

"After your phone call the other night, we decided to go back to that house, you know, the one with all the dead bodies?"

"Just the two of them," I insisted.

"Everything was as we found it the first time, no dead bodies, no sign of a struggle, no bullet holes, nothing. Everything was at it should have been . . . except for a set of fingerprints."

I tried to look O'Neal straight in the eye.

"We ran a check on them and discovered they belonged to somebody by the name of Tony Blake. Does that name ring any bells with you, Mr Mahoney?"

I had walked headlong into O'Neal's trap. There was no way out and O'Neal knew it. I was convinced that only the drift of cigarette smoke clinging to O'Neal's throat kept him from smirking at me again.

"Should it?" I asked.

The Sergeant sat down and folded his hands in front of him on the table.

"He lives in Manchester."

"Since when was that a crime?"

"We asked some questions and it turns out he came to Scarborough to write a book."

"Now that might be!"

O'Neal leaned forward and whispered, "You know what I think, Mr Mahoney?"

"I'm sure I couldn't contain the excitement if I did!"

"This man, Tony Blake, travels to Scarborough to write a book. Trouble is, at the end of the day, he realises that nothing ever happens here so he decides to take matters into his own hands . . ."

I laughed. Not a lot, just enough to let him know how ridiculous he sounded.

"You think that this guy, Tony Blake, goes around killing people just so he can write a book?"

"All he needs is the motive."

"And what is the motive?"

But O'Neal didn't answer. He simply got to his feet, picked up the file and headed for the door. I watched Matthews stub out his cigarette on the floor with the heel of his shoe. He stared at me for a moment then followed O'Neal.

I sprang up and made for the door, blocking his way.

"You don't seriously go along with all that, do you?"

Matthews looked at me and slowly shook his head. "When Sergeant O'Neal first came to me with the idea, I laughed, very much like you just did."

I felt relieved but only until Matthews took hold of the door and looked back at me.

"But that was before he told me about the five-hundred-thousand pound advance Tony Blake had been offered for his book!"

~

They left me waiting another twenty minutes before a policewoman entered and said I could go. Just like that. I looked at her without moving a muscle as the alternatives slipped through my head. The first was ridiculous, like in the movies when they offer the prisoner the chance to run so that they can shoot him in the back. The second was far more realistic, that they just didn't have enough to keep me there any longer. But the third was more plausible. They would tail me, hoping I'd make a fatal slip, something that would give them all they needed to arrest me.

A bright red sky hung over the station as I stepped outside to the sound of clinking milk bottles and the whistling of a postmen. I hadn't slept a wink all night. My breath stank, my clothes stank, my life stank.

I went back to the guest house, showered, changed my clothes, looked at the television, thought about what to do next and fell asleep.

~

I woke to the sound of breaking glass. I jumped up, pulled back the curtains and caught sight of a small group of teenagers pointing fingers at one another, insisting that, if they hadn't had so much to drink, they'd really do something other than call one another names.

It was five-thirty. I'd been asleep for over twelve hours. It was the most I'd slept in ages and it felt good. But good was all I felt. In a little over two hours Short Suit and Nails would come looking for me . . .

~

I stood inside a battered bike shed adjacent to the library and watched as people came and went. First Ms Simms, then Gerald and Sophie. Finally Trish appeared in a roll-neck sweater and jeans. I stepped out in front of her.

"I need to talk to you."

She wasn't impressed.

"I'm in trouble!"

She raised an eyebrow.

"Can we go somewhere? . . . Please!"

We walked side by side to the Secret Garden, which, despite its name was anything but secret and didn't look much like a garden. I ordered two coffees and we sat at a table.

"What kind of trouble are you in? And am I going to regret asking?"

"Are you always so blunt? I haven't even finished sugaring my drink."

"That stuff isn't very good for you!"

I looked at the sugar as it trickled from my spoon.

"I used to think the same thing," I said, "but now it's the least of my worries."

Trish was looking at me and it was a worried look. It wondered what on earth she was getting herself involved in and why.

And, much as I tried to think otherwise, I couldn't help wondering the same thing. I didn't even know her. I hadn't invited her here so that she could come up with some sweeping words of wisdom or wonderful quote from Chandler that would help me see this case in a new light. I'd invited her here because I fancied her and I was kind of hoping that the feeling was mutual.

I was wrong.

"Look, I'm sorry. I shouldn't have . . . I mean, you don't really need to get involved."

Trish went to take a sip of her drink but it must have been too hot. She placed her cup back down and looked at me.

"You've brought me this far, you might as well take me the rest of the way."

Somehow it still didn't seem right, but she was a big girl now and surely old enough to look after herself.

"This book I've been writing . . ."

She nodded.

"Well, it's not so much a book, it's more of a diary."

Trish focussed her gaze on me.

"Everything I talked about in the Writers' Circle actually happened, the bodies, the missing people and me playing at being a Private Investigator, it's all for real."

But Trish didn't appear surprised or even shocked. In fact she didn't appear anything at all. That caught me off guard. I mean, shouldn't she have been the slightest bit concerned?

"And now the police want to pin the whole thing on me." I added.

Trish raised an eyebrow. It was the first hint that I hadn't just been talking to myself.

"They know about my book, they know I've been offered a five-hundred-thousand pound advance, and they think that's reason enough for me to go round killing people."

Trish pressed a finger to her lips and glanced across the room.

"I can see why that would be a very good motive," she said.

"I was kind of hoping you'd be on my side!"

"Is that what you want, me to be on your side?"

I shrugged my shoulders.

"I don't know." I said, finally. "I guess I just wanted somebody to talk to, somebody who didn't want me either in jail or dead."

"Dead?"

"Yeah, there are these goons who want some prints I took from Fitzsimmons' house. Trouble is I haven't got them any more."

"What happened to them?"

"I left them in a shop to be developed and of course, as happens when you leave something in a shop to be developed, it got burnt down."

"They were destroyed?"

"The whole place was destroyed."

I don't know why but I found myself looking at her hands. There were no rings on her fingers and that was a sign, a very bad sign. It meant I had no real reason not to ask her out, apart from the fact that being a real bad PI could get me killed before she got the chance to slap my face.

"Why do you think they destroyed the shop?" she asked.

"I don't know, I mean it doesn't make sense, one day they're ransacking my office, the next they're destroying a shop."

Trish pushed her cup to one side and leant towards me.

"There are two possibilities as far as I can see," she said. "One, there's more than just these people you mentioned after the prints."

"And two?"

"That whoever was after the prints couldn't find them, so they destroyed the shop, assuming that if they couldn't have them, nobody could."

"Yes, but . . ."

Trish raised a finger at me.

"So they can't be one hundred per cent sure that the prints were actually destroyed."

It was possible that what she was saying made sense, it was just that I was having a whole load of trouble keeping up with her.

Trish sat back in her chair. She had the look of someone who was dying to be asked what was on her mind.

"What's on your mind?"

"You have a choice. You can either hope that the people you referred to are sure that they destroyed the prints and therefore won't be back to bother you."

"Or?"

"You can pretend that you still have them and lure them into a trap."

I took a minute to look around the room as if searching for inspiration but all I could see was plastic flowers and naked statues.

"All I ever seem to do is end up pretending everything," my voice sounded drained.

"Maybe that's what you're good at."

I looked at Trish. If her face had been a mirror I'm sure I'd have seen an anxious expression staring back at me.

"Maybe I'd better be!" I said.

How about a third choice? How about the two of us ran away together and sod the consequences? Sod the book, sod the case. Sod everything.

We walked out onto the precinct. Trish checked her watch.

"Are you going in?" I asked, nodding towards the library.

She shook her head.

"You don't like it that much anyway!"

She almost smiled. "It's like watching one of those really awful films; you keep looking because you can't believe it will get any worse."

"I couldn't have put it better myself."

Trish looked at me. "So what are you going to do now?"

I shrugged my shoulders. "Well, running and hiding came a close second, but I think I'll go and see Walker."

"The Inspector?"

I nodded.

"You can't be too sure that he's not involved."

That wasn't what I wanted to hear.

"I don't suppose I can be sure of anything any more."

Trish smiled. "Well at least there's one good thing."

"There is?"

"At least you'll have a good book."

"As long as I don't end up in jail, or dead, first!"

~

I found Walker working out in the gym. I wasn't happy about having to pay three quid just to spend five minutes with someone who didn't even want me there. And I wasn't happy about having to borrow a pair of track-suit bottoms two sizes too big for me either.

The room was wide and long and packed with people of all shapes and sizes. People who would never lose weight even if they ran to China and back, and others who spent their time in love with their reflections in the huge plate-glass mirrors everywhere.

Walker was sitting on an exercise bike. He wasn't pedalling hard, but with just enough power to force lines of sweat to trickle down his face. A matchstick was clamped tightly between his teeth. He wasn't happy to see me. I wasn't surprised.

"Christ, can't I even work out in peace?"

I smiled and straddled the bike next to his. "There's something I've got to tell you."

"And I'm not going to like it, am I?" he grunted.

I gave Walker time to towel his face.

"The night I found Fitzsimmons, or at least the night I claim to have found him . . ."

Walker nodded.

"I found something else as well."

Walker rolled a frown at me. "What something?"

"Two strips of film negatives."

"Of what?"

"I don't know. I couldn't make them out, so I took them to be developed."

"Go on!" He sounded angry.

"The shop was gutted . . . that's the bit you're not going to like."

"I would never have guessed it! And when did all this happen?"

"Yesterday."

Walker brought the edge of his fist down towards the handlebars but stopped just short of slamming it hard down. "I knew it," he said. "I just knew it. I knew you were keeping something back. And let me guess, the negatives were ruined?"

"It looks like it."

Walker's face was like thunder. "So that's it?" he snapped. "You come in here to tell me you've stolen evidence and that, thanks to your interfering in a police investigation, they're destroyed!"

I stared across the room and stayed silent.

Walker's glare pounded me into submission. "Tell me, Mahoney, were you born unlucky, or are you just having a bad week?"

I ignored the remark and fixed my gaze on the computer screen in front of the bike. I pressed a couple of buttons and two men began racing one another. The man in black pulled away and I realised it wasn't me. He looked like a man possessed. I stepped up my pace but it didn't make any difference. I'd have needed a motorbike to keep up.

I glanced at Walker. "Look, I don't see what you're getting all sore about, it was only the other day you were convinced I was making all this up!"

"Yeah, well, I'm entitled to change my mind."

"Well, maybe if you'd changed it a little earlier I would have come to you with the negatives."

Walker raised his hand and for a moment appeared to accept the point.

"Anyway," I continued.

"Don't tell me there's more?"

"I think the fire was started deliberately."

"That's all very well, but you don't have a clue who by, do you! Do you?"

"No! But I reckon whoever it was wanted to destroy the negatives and the prints."

"You think somebody was after them?"

"I know somebody was after them! They trashed Ronnie's office."

Walker slowed his pace and looked at me with an expression verging on intrigue.

"And I think they're the same people who worked me over the other night."

"You told me that was just a fight!"

"Like I said, I didn't see the point in telling you anything considering you haven't believed a damn word I've said all week!"

"So why are you telling me now?"

I was slow to answer.

"Why are you telling me now?" he repeated.

I looked at the screen. The man in black was so far ahead that all there was left for me to do was shoot him. "Can I trust you, Walker?"

He almost laughed aloud at the notion that I might think otherwise.

"Look, I know what you must be thinking, Mahoney, and I don't blame you. I've been a pain in the arse from the word go. But I don't like what I've seen and I want to get to the bottom of it just like you do."

"I reckon whoever burnt down the shop did it because they couldn't get their hands on the negatives . . ."

"So you said."

I raised a finger to suggest I was about to get to the point. "So they can't be certain they were destroyed, can they?"

Walker sat back and chewed on the matchstick, thinking. "You're going to call their bluff, is that it?"

I nodded and Walker smiled. I thought it was because he liked the idea.

"It's amazing," he said. "I've only known you about a week but that has to be the most ridiculous idea you've had yet!"

I tried not to appear put out. "Actually I can't take all the credit for this one."

"Don't tell me there's somebody else involved?"

"Not exactly, she's just somebody I spoke to."

"You mean you told her everything?"

I didn't like his tone, it sounded critical and I wasn't in the mood for being criticised.

"I take it she's pretty?"

Nor was that the conversation I'd had planned. But then again, I couldn't really argue. Trish was pretty and I had told her everything. I stopped pedalling.

"What's her name?"

"What?"

"What's her name?"

"Trish."

"And?"

"And nothing."

"How well do you know her?"

I had no idea why Walker was asking me and I had even less idea why I wanted to answer him. "I don't. I mean other than we met at the Writers' Circle, she's got high cheekbones and she can quote Chandler."

"Sounds like the perfect recipe for romance!"

"I wouldn't know." I mumbled. "Why all the questions?"

Walker started to chew his match. "It's my job."

"Liar!"

"Then maybe I'm worried."

"About what?" I asked.

"About the fact that yesterday these prints were history as far as you were concerned and now, somebody you hardly know suddenly wants you to pretend that they still exist."

"She's just trying to help!" I replied, a little more defensively than I'd intended.

"Yes, but who?"

I got off my bike. I hadn't gone far but I looked like I'd taken a shower.

"You've got cynical in your old age, Walker!"

The Inspector smiled. "I was always cynical!"

"Or maybe you just don't like the fact that I've found somebody I can trust."

"No. Maybe I don't like the idea that you think you can trust anybody at all."

~

I went back to the guest house, showered and changed. I figured if I was going to die I might as well look good about it. A shirt, tie, neatly pressed trousers and some money in my pocket. At least that way, if I wound up dead, the police might care enough to investigate.

I called into the shop. The old man was there fumbling through a cardboard box. I tapped on the door frame and the old man squinted at me as I made my way across the rotten floorboards.

"You're the fella who works for Ronnie!"

I nodded. He still didn't know he was dead.

"What can I do for you?"

"It's about those prints."

"Well like I told you . . ."

"I know. Look, I'd like to pay you for them anyway." I handed him an envelope. He looked at the money, then at me, and his face was a picture of puzzles.

"I don't understand, there's far too much here."

"Look, let's just say I feel responsible for what happened here."

"You mean . . ."

"It's possible somebody was after those prints I gave you. So how about you treat yourself and your old lady to a nice holiday somewhere."

He looked back at the envelope and didn't seem to know what to say. I turned to leave.

"Oh, and by the way, if anybody comes asking questions, tell them everything you know."

"But I don't know anything!" he exclaimed.

"That'll do nicely."

I returned to the office and unlocked the door. I left the light off and sat at the desk. Only the flicker of a neon light outside and the hum of traffic disturbed the tranquillity.

I unscrewed the whisky bottle and poured myself a shot. What had seemed like a good idea an hour ago was now starting to worry me. All week long I'd been stumbling blindly into problems. That wasn't so bad, but now I was inviting them in through the front door and I had no idea who, or what, was about to turn up.

I'd laid my cards on the table, now all they had to do was come up trumps . . . fat chance!

17

The clock on the wall said three-fifteen. I hadn't even noticed it wasn't working. I thought about fixing it but couldn't be bothered. There didn't seem much point. I wasn't in any rush for seven o'clock to arrive.

I spun my chair round and stared out of the window into the darkness that was gathering over the sea, wrapping itself around a lonely fishing boat struggling home towards the harbour.

Where did I go wrong? Was it tipping back that whisky the other night? Answering the phone the following morning? Or falling for Helen Fitzsimmons and her deep brown eyes? I'd been stupid enough to think it was important and that I was big enough to work it out when all the time I was just plain dumb. That's what happens to dumb people. They get punished while the criminals walk free.

A streak of lightning lit up the horizon and the creak of a floorboard preceded a voice from the past. "Time's up, Mahoney!"

It was Short Suit and he didn't have to pull the trigger for me to know he was holding a gun to the back of my neck.

"Where are the prints?"

"I haven't got them."

He pressed the gun harder into my neck.

I sat up slowly and tried to look as if I wasn't bothered.

"You're lying!"

"Are you sure?"

Out in the street somebody slammed a car door and my heart skipped a beat. It wasn't the smartest thing to say to someone holding a gun to my head. Unfortunately it was the truth. The car started up and pulled away. For a moment there was nothing but silence, flashing neons and Short Suit's bad breath.

In that moment of silence I wondered how it would be. Would I get one last chance like in the movies, or would he just pull the trigger and that would be that? And while I wondered he withdrew the cold barrel and stepped out in front of me.

He was just as I remembered him. He hadn't changed a bit. And by that I mean he hadn't changed a bit. He was wearing the same black suit, and the same rolled-up cigarette dangled from between his lips. Whoever he was working for, they weren't paying him enough.

"How much longer do you think you can go on calling my bluff, Mahoney?"

"Just as long as you have no idea what's going on."

He hunched his shoulders and waved the gun at me like a sparkler. "Maybe I don't care what's going on. Maybe I should just shoot you here and now."

"Then you'll never know what happened to the negatives."

"Well, I've been thinking about that," he said. "I think you've been lying all along. I don't think you've got the negatives at all. I think they were destroyed in a fire."

"That's a lot of thinking!"

His face twitched ever so slightly. "And even if they weren't destroyed, there's not too many places you could hide them."

"Unless I've passed them on to someone else, of course!" I suggested. It was my last throw of the dice. The one I prayed would come up sixes. The one that either had me smiling or left with a shirt full of holes.

"Like who?" he snarled.

"The cops," I said.

He started laughing and waving the gun around, repeating the word 'cops' over and over. I didn't like the way he said it. I didn't like the way he made it sound like it was a four-letter word. Like it was the kind of word you wouldn't use in front of your mother.

Then he stopped laughing and aimed the gun at my chest.

"Time to say your prayers, Mahoney."

It was a natural reaction. The phone rang and we both looked at it. But while I was able to look at it straight on, he had to crank his neck round and it was all I needed. I leapt up and clasped my hand around the barrel of the gun. We danced like pigeons across the room, twisting the gun this way and that until his back was pressed against the wall. I tried to flip him, but only succeeded in lobbing the gun across the floor and landing on top of him. We were face to face. He stretched out a hand and wrapped his fingers across the bridge of my nose. It felt like he was about to tear my head off.

I could see the gun out of the corner of my eye. It was only a few yards away, but as I reached out I lost my balance and he flicked me onto my back. From that moment on things went from bad to worse. When he wasn't smacking my head against the floor, he was denting his knuckles with my face.

And then, like it mattered, I realised the phone had stopped ringing and I wondered who it was and if they'd ring back .

My skull was coming apart at the seams. I made one last desperate grab for the gun, my fingers kissing the tip of the barrel. Short Suit squeezed his fingers around my neck. He was enjoying himself - the bastard. My head started to swell, my eyes bulged. I could hardly breathe. I stretched out again and caught hold of the gun's barrel. The room was growing darker. I pulled it towards me and pointed it at his face. He let go of my throat and pressed the muzzle of the gun back towards me. It was the only thing going my way.

My fingers were trapped around the trigger. I could feel the blood seeping from them as his grip tightened. The gun swung like a pendulum backwards and forwards between the two of us until . . . finally, it went off.

Short Suit was still smiling, but his eyes looked like they were about to implode. They rolled up and around their sockets, and he flopped down on top of me.

I pushed and kicked and heaved him over to one side. He fell with a bump to the floor. Face down on the ground, he lay very still. Smoke filtered up from the gun. I got up and dropped it onto the floor. I rubbed my hands and massaged some feeling back into my fingers.

Short Suit looked like he was dead. I was relieved it wasn't me. I'd come so close. But I was supposed to be a PI. I was meant to solve problems, not go around shooting people when all else failed.

Not that I got the time to drift into a moral debate with myself because the feeling had just begun to return to my fingers when Nails appeared in the doorway looking more than a little upset. Most of the light filtering in from the hallway was eclipsed by his bulk. He glanced down at the floor, at his partner and then across at me with a cruel, payback expression in his eyes.

I lunged for the gun and pointed it at him. My hand was shaking.

"Hold it right there, or I'll shoot."

I might as well have asked him to dance the tango for all the good it did because he just came straight at me, his size thirteens pounding the floor.

I squeezed the trigger, more from fear than intent. The first shot caught him in the left shoulder. It stopped him in his tracks as he inspected the wound. He grinned, fixed me with that cruel smile again and carried on walking.

I steadied my hand and fired again. This time I hit him in the stomach. He took a step back and clasped both massive hands to his midriff. But even that didn't stop him . . .

By the time I'd emptied the magazine he was standing over me, arms aloft, ready to strike me down with one fatal blow. I was pressed up against the window when he fell like a giant redwood and crashed to the floor. The desk shook, the room shook, the whole damn street shook.

I looked at the gun in my hand and swore to myself that next time I would use a catapult.

The dust had just started to settle when I heard a groan from Short Suit. I crouched next to him and pushed back his shoulder till I could see his face. Blood was seeping through his shirt and spilling onto the floor. I checked the blood. It was real and it was going to stain the carpet. Nobody was going to catch me out this time.

He opened his eyes. "Call me an ambulance."

"I don't think calling you names is going to help right now, but telling me who wanted those negatives might!"

"I don't know what you're talking about."

"No, that's my line, you have to tell me the truth."

"Go to hell."

I stood up. "Fine, and if you're lucky the cleaner will find you sometime tomorrow."

"You wouldn't dare," he moaned. But the exertion had him reaching down to where the bullet had entered. He cradled the pain in the palm of his hand.

"So tell me who the negatives were for!"

"You don't want to know."

I pressed my hand hard across the back of his.

His eyes widened in excruciating pain. "You bastard!"

I pressed harder.

"All right. All right!"

I released my hand.

"I got a note from someone."

"Who?"

"I don't know. They didn't leave a name. It just said they needed a job doing."

"How did they pay you?"

"Via a box number."

"And what did they tell you about me?"

"That you had some negatives that belonged to them."

"Is that all?"

"And that we had to get them back, one way or another."

"And you have no idea what they were pictures of?"

"What do I care, just so long as I get paid!"

"So how do I find him, whoever he is?"

"You don't have to worry about that . . . they'll find you!"

I let go of his hand and stood up.

He twisted his head up towards me. "You're a dead man, Mahoney, you mark my words."

"That's good coming from the guy who's bleeding to death on the floor."

"Believe me, you'd have done yourself a favour if you'd let me shoot you."

I wasn't sure what to make of that threat. But it didn't really matter. His lips had only just stopped moving when the phone rang again.

"Hello."

There was a momentary pause and then a voice asked, "Mr Mahoney?"

"That depends . . . who's asking?"

"It's me, Roger Laughton."

I checked my watch. "Shouldn't you be in bed counting all your money?"

Laughton coughed. I couldn't be sure if he was playing it for real or for effect.

"I've been considering what you said the other day."

"I said a lot of things the other day."

"About doing something useful, and . . ." The old man paused.

"And?"

"This idea that Helen had, about somebody blackmailing me, I think I know who it might be."

"Who?"

"Or maybe I should say, I think I know why someone might be blackmailing me."

"Go on."

"A short time ago, I made it known that I was opposed to these new plans for the old south bay swimming pool."

"Yeah, you figured it would be bad for business!"

"Actually I wasn't thinking of myself this time."

"So surprise me!"

"Well how do you think a Mickey Mouse theme park would have looked next to a Victorian grand hall? It's simply a matter of taste, Mr Mahoney and not building something on the cheap just to bring in a little trade."

"So what happened?"

"Nothing. I mean, the building went ahead as you know . . . until the landslide."

"So what's that got to do with you being blackmailed?"

"After the hotel collapsed I made it known that I wanted to sell the land to the National Trust. I didn't want the council getting their hands on it, for fear of what they might turn it into."

"And they didn't like that?"

"I'm only guessing, but shortly after that I received the note."

"But what is it they had on you?"

Laughton stalled on a cough.

"What is it they had on you, Laughton?"

"Shortly after my son died I had some work done on the hotel he left behind."

"Yeah, The Gables, I know about it."

The old man seemed surprised that I knew as much. "Well some of the work included an extension to the rear."

"I'm listening."

"That was the first part of the hotel to collapse."

I heard another cough, only longer and harder this time. "This is very difficult for me, Mr Mahoney."

"More difficult than having your daughter die on you?"

There was a pause and I thought the old man was going to hang up on me. But I could still hear him wheezing so I figured he was just pulling faces at me.

"The extension came without any planning permission."

Interesting.

"Maybe somebody's got it into their head that you're responsible for the accident?"

Laughton coughed.

"Was there an investigation?"

"No, nothing official anyway. Some men came up from the council one day, just to see what needed to be done."

"And nobody asked any questions?"

"Not that I know of."

"Mmm," I mused, holding the phone in one hand and pulling my ear with the other.

"What is it, Mr Mahoney? Do you know who's responsible?"

"Not exactly," I replied. "But I know a man who might."

I hung up and rang the council. I needed to speak to Frank Hebden. A featureless voice asked me to hold. I said I hadn't time and could I ring back in an hour? The voice said no, because Mr Hebden was due to leave in twenty minutes. That was all I needed to know.

Short Suit was still clutching his stomach and staring up at me like a cat round an empty bowl. I phoned the police and asked for Walker. But he wasn't at his desk.

"Would you like to leave a message?"

"Yeah. Just tell him Mahoney called and that it's urgent, I'm going up to the Gables Hotel, he can find me there. Oh, and by the way . . . there's someone in my office bleeding to death."

~

The voice on the phone had lied. It was another half hour before Hebden left his office. It was dark and rain had started to fall. He hurried to his car without a mind for anyone or anything. I followed a few steps behind and waited until he unlocked the door. Then I drew the empty gun and dug it into his ribs.

"Get in," I said.

Hebden looked at the gun and then at me with eyes the size of dinner plates.

"Mr Mahoney!"

I gritted my teeth.

"Get in and unlock the back door!"

Hebden did as I said. I climbed into the back and put the gun back in my pocket.

"Now drive!"

"But . . ."

"Just drive!"

He tried to start the engine. It took three attempts, but I put it down to

142

nerves. It's not easy trying to be impressive when there's a gun aimed at you.

"Where to?" he asked.

"Just make a right at the gates. That's all you need to know for now."

"Actually you're wrong, Mr Mahoney. There's a lot I need to know, like why are you pointing a gun at me?"

"All in good time, Mr Hebden, all in good time."

~

Lightning crackled through the blackened sky, lighting up the horizon and silhouetting the high wire fence surrounding The Gables. We came to a stop beneath a large 'KEEP OUT' sign and through the hazy glare of the headlights I watched the rain pound down on the concrete rubble beyond.

I told Hebden to turn off the engine and picked up a torch.

"Get out."

The torch flickered and died leaving us in the sheets of lightning which broke overhead.

"Come on! Stupid thing!" I shook the torch until it came back on and told Hebden to start moving. We circled the fence until we found a gap. I pulled back the wire and waited for him to squeeze through. I quickly followed. All the time I pointed the empty gun at him.

I nodded in the direction of the brick and timber remains of what had been a thriving hotel. A door swinging on a hinge led us into a room with hanging cupboards and walls at forty-five degree angles. I aimed the torch at a floor of broken glass, rotting timber, mouldering carpets and a pool of water swiftly gathering at the lower end of the room.

The torch died and left us in darkness. I shook it again and it sprang back to life.

Thunder rumbled angrily outside.

"All right. You can stop right there, Hebden."

"Mind telling me what's going on, Mahoney?"

I shone the torch into his face. The light wasn't very bright but he held a hand in front of his eyes to shield them from the glare. "Actually, I was hoping you'd tell me."

"I don't understand."

"It's simple. Roger Laughton recently spent a lot of dough doing up this hotel. It came with an extension, this extension, an extension he didn't get planning permission for."

Hebden frowned.

The torch started to fade again. I shook it and aimed it back at Hebden.

"I still don't understand. We can't keep tabs on everybody, if that's what you're suggesting."

I shook my head. "I appreciate that. Except when a hotel collapses and kills one of the guests, then I'd expect you to start asking questions."

Hebden's frown disappeared. He looked down at the gun in my hand. "You've got the wrong department."

"Come on, Hebden, this isn't about departments, this is about Roger Laughton and everything he stands for. You hate the guy, he's one of the reasons nothing ever gets done around here, you said so yourself."

Hebden brushed back the hair from his forehead with the back of his hand and smiled. It wasn't a confident smile, just a smile. "A few years ago you might have had a point, Mr Mahoney. A few years ago I might have cared less. But not now, not any more. This town's drained every last breath from me. I don't care what happens to it any more."

"So you did nothing?"

"I heard rumours, but none of them made any difference. If it wasn't Laughton wagging his greedy finger it was someone else."

"So you weren't trying to blackmail him?"

"For what? Everybody knows he's on his knees. There wouldn't have been any point."

"There was to me!"

I was looking at Hebden, but his lips hadn't moved.

The voice had come from the summer breeze standing just behind me.

I turned to see Mandy Woodhall soaked to the skin. She didn't look like someone who planned on spending the night with two men in a tumbledown hotel on a wet and windy cliff top.

Normally I would have been pleased to see her, but normally she wouldn't have been pointing a gun at my stomach . . .

She dug it into my ribs and forced me to drop my gun and move over next to Hebden. We stood with our backs to the wall, watching the rain pour through the ravaged ceiling, wondering what would happen next.

"Aren't you going to ask?" she smiled.

"Ask?"

"What a nice girl like me is doing in a place like this."

"It had crossed my mind."

She stepped up close to me, close enough to run the tip of the barrel down the side of my face. "I was counting on you, Tony."

I repeated the word 'counting' a couple of times to myself. The impact of it was like hitting me with a hammer. "You've been using me?"

"Oh, you make it sound so harsh, but you were doing such a good job.

Better than Ronnie anyway."

Hebden pointed a finger skywards. "Wait a minute. I thought your name was Richard?"

"It's a long story," I sighed. "And one that neither of us is going to like."

Mandy smiled. "You see, Tony isn't a real detective, he's just writing a book, a very good book perhaps, but he's been deceiving us all, all along. Pretty good, don't you think!"

"But not half as pretty or half as good as you!" I said.

A gust of wind shook what was left of the walls but Mandy didn't seem to notice. She was still staring at me and smiling.

"So it was you who was blackmailing Laughton?"

Mandy nodded.

"With what?"

She shrugged. "Nothing really. I didn't have a lot to go on other than that the cliff was unsafe and the hotel had fallen into the sea. He was a powerful man, and powerful men have a habit of upsetting a lot of people along the way."

"You were calling his bluff?"

"Clever, don't you think!"

Personally I did think it was clever, very clever, but then I'm not very clever.

Hebden was growing impatient and the swaying roof was making him increasingly nervous.

"What the hell's any of this got to do with me?" he yelled.

Mandy kissed me on the cheek and stepped in front of Hebden. There was a confident air about the way she spoke and the way she held the gun. And that was enough for me.

"I want to know why the council didn't do as I asked."

"I don't know what you're talking about!"

She pressed the gun into Hebden's face. "Not good enough!"

"I had nothing to do with it, I swear it!"

"I'm going to count to three."

"She's crazy."

"That doesn't take a lot of working out when someone's pointing a gun at your head," I said.

"One."

Hebden's eyes were dancing the tango as he shuffled from one foot to another like someone impatiently waiting for a bus . . .

"Two . . ."

"Use your gun, Mahoney. Use it now!"

I looked down at the gun and smiled. "Wouldn't do much good, Hebden, it's empty."

Hebden looked back at Mandy. His eyes narrowed. He wasn't happy. "What the hell do you want to know for anyway?"

Mandy brushed her lips to his ear.

"Remember the old lady that died in the accident?"

Hebden nodded.

"And the old man who died shortly after of a broken heart?"

Hebden nodded again.

"They were my parents!"

For a moment there was silence, filled only with the pouring rain, the howling wind and the waves beating on the rocks far below.

I was stuck in a room with a beautiful girl pointing a gun at an innocent man, but all I could think of was the brief moments we'd spent together in Spillanes and at the office, with her healing hands and perfect lips. I had been on the crest of a wave whilst she pulled my strings. The word mug was written all over my forehead.

I glanced at Hebden. Mandy's gun was practically twisting his nose halfway up his face. He was backed uncomfortably up against the wall. I suddenly felt sorry for him.

"Two and a half . . ."

The roof swayed alarmingly under the weight of the wind and rain. It was time to do something desperate.

"Look, Mandy, if you're going to shoot him, you'd better get it over with. This place is going to come down on us like a ton of bricks any minute now."

Hebden briefly took his eyes from the gun and shot me a despairing glance.

"But you know that wouldn't be right, don't you? You know the only thing pulling that trigger will achieve is a great big hole in Hebden's face."

"Perhaps it's what he deserves."

"And what about your parents? Don't you think they deserve a proper explanation?"

"What's the point? They always cover everything up!"

Her hand was shaking so much I was afraid the gun would go off accidentally.

"No, not this time . . . I've got proof."

It wasn't much, but it was enough to grab her attention. She stole a glance at me out of the corner of her eye.

"What do you mean?"

"I mean I have the negatives and the prints."

Mandy froze. The gun was perched on Hebden's face, but the earlier ice-cold glare in her eyes had subsided. I took a step forward and reached for the gun.

Her hand stopped shaking.

Hebden was breathing heavily, sweat trickling down his furrowed brow as his eyes stayed fixed on the muzzle of the gun.

"We'll go about things the proper way," I said calmly.

My fingers were about to tip the barrel of the gun just as she pulled back.

"No. I don't trust you, I don't trust any of you!"

She aimed the gun at Hebden.

"Including yourself?" I asked.

"What . . . what are you talking about?"

"You need someone to blame for your parents' death, otherwise you'd have to blame yourself!"

Mandy stepped back just far enough to point the gun at the pair of us.

I'd managed to talk myself into a whole lot of trouble.

"What's all that got to do with me?"

"You told me you did the survey, you discovered the cliff wasn't safe, yet you let your parents stay in a hotel just two hundred yards away . . ."

"I had no idea it would collapse!"

"Maybe you didn't, but it hasn't stopped you from wondering, has it?" I couldn't even be sure that what I was saying made any sense, but I was desperate. But whatever it was that I'd touched on made Mandy drop her guard.

She looked at the floor in painful recollection and the gun loosened in her hand.

I put my arm around her and didn't even see Hebden move. One minute he was saying his prayers, the next he had taken the gun from Mandy.

He shoved the two of us roughly against the wall and was his old confident self again. There was a glint in the back of his eyes as he held out a hand. "Now, give me the negatives and the prints, Mahoney."

"Oh no, not again."

"Give them to me!"

I looked at Hebden and thought that this shouldn't be happening.

"You're not going to believe me, Hebden, but I haven't got them."

"Don't lie to me!"

"I told you."

Hebden lashed out, cracking me around the side of the head with the butt of the gun. I stumbled, but didn't fall. My face was ablaze, my head shrieking in pain.

"You just said . . ."

"I was trying to save your miserable life, you idiot!" Now I was angry.

Hebden looked confused, trapped between wanting to thank me and aching to shoot me. "So where are they?"

I wiped blood from my lip. But the pause was long enough for him to hit me again.

I really didn't like Hebden now.

"Where are they?"

"They were destroyed in a fire."

"You're lying!"

"So everybody keeps telling me."

Hebden took a step back and wiped the rain from his face. He needed time to think.

"Did you see what was on them?"

I shook my head. "They were no good. The guy in the shop said he could improve them, but he never got around to doing it."

Hebden appeared thoughtful for a moment and I wondered what was going around in his crazy head and how much trouble it could be for me.

"That's too bad, Mahoney," he said with a smile. He aimed the gun at me and I couldn't help thinking that he knew how to use it. I mean, he wasn't about to pull the trigger and suddenly yell, 'Fore!'

"Don't I at least get to know why you're going to kill me?"

"This isn't the movies, Mahoney!"

I flicked off the torch and the place went black. Hebden fired a shot but I didn't feel a thing. I pushed past him and made for the nearest door. I had no idea where it led, but as shots rang out behind me I didn't care. A stone staircase opened up below me. It seemed to curl away forever. I fingered my way down along the walls until I came out into what appeared to be a tunnel.

There was the sound of heavy footsteps close behind me.

"Mahoney?"

It was Hebden. I let his words fall into the silence and the rain as I made my way along the tunnel as fast as I dared. In the distance I could hear the sound of waves crashing against the rocks.

Hebden called out again. He was getting closer. An alcove of sorts suddenly loomed up on the right just as Hebden pointed the torch in my direction. I stepped inside and pressed myself tight against the wall. The light flickered and died.

"Bloody thing!" Hebden mumbled.

I heard what appeared to be the wrench of a lever and suddenly a humming sound filled the tunnel and a row of lights spilt the darkness. The walls were supported by creaking wooden pillars that leaked dripping water into squelchy pools of mud. Large wooden crates had been stacked on either side of the tunnel. It wasn't a nice place to be. It was cold and dark and it stank of seaweed and salt.

"Like what you see, Mahoney?" Hebden yelled.

I didn't answer. He knew I was down there but he didn't know where. I looked to my right. The tunnel disappeared into the darkness. There was no way out.

"You're standing in a smuggler's tunnel. Some of the stuff in those crates is over three hundred years old. It's treasure, Mahoney, real treasure."

Hebden was drawing closer. I inched my feet out of the mud and eased back further into the darkness as he passed by and continued down the main tunnel.

"Funny thing is I've been waiting years for a chance like this, something to put this town back on the map. We'd have had television crews here, archaeologists, even tourists; and this time people like Laughton wouldn't have had them all to themselves . . ."

"So what's stopping you?"

Hebden paused as if trying to decide where my voice had come from. Then I heard his footsteps squelch in the mud. He was heading in the wrong direction.

"Two things," he continued. "A couple of years ago people reported a hole in the cliff face, it was thought to be a collapsed sewer pipe. I gave the order to have it blocked off, I just couldn't see the point in spending all that money on filling in a hole. That was my big mistake . . ."

"Is that what caused the landslip?" I put to him.

He paused again. "Possibly," he agreed. "But then again, I couldn't see what all the fuss was about, I mean it's hardly the San Andreas fault and people build whole cities on that. What do you say to that, Mahoney?"

I was already edging my way slowly back towards the tunnel. Rain was leaking in everywhere. The timber supports were slowly giving way, subsiding into the mud.

"I'd say that when somebody dies it's worth making a fuss."

"That's all people do is fuss. You've got to wrap them up in cotton wool nowadays or they end up suing you. Nobody wants to do anything for themselves any more."

"Is that why you couldn't afford an investigation, because the council would have been sued?"

"Sod the council, I could have been charged with manslaughter!"

"That's what was on the negatives, isn't it? Proof that you blocked off the hole."

"I presume so. But now they've been destroyed they won't resurface again!"

"So why go on killing? Without those negatives it's just my word against yours and you're a respected councillor. I'm just a part-time nobody."

"You belittle yourself, Mr Mahoney. You're a very dedicated man who has worked very hard to discover the truth."

From out of nowhere Hebden suddenly appeared behind me. He was still holding the gun and smiling.

"And look where it's got me!" I mumbled.

"You won't give up, that's both your gift and your flaw. Sooner or later you'll find something and I just can't afford to let that happen."

"And what's going to happen to all this?"

Hebden inched closer to me. His eyes were literally on fire with avarice. "Finders keepers."

"You really don't care about the town any more do you?"

He laughed hysterically. "All this lousy town has ever done is pull me under. Well it's got another think coming now. I'm going to have my name in lights, Mahoney. People are going read about me, see my picture all over the place and know I was the man who saved this lousy town and its ungrateful people . . ."

"Even Helen?"

Hebden stopped laughing. "I was ready to give that woman everything. I loved her more than any man could, but she never looked twice at me. Women like her don't look at men like me. Little men, men of no substance, no power . . ."

"And now you're happy to bump people off?"

Hebden narrowed his eyes. "Bump people off? I haven't bumped anybody off."

"No! What about Eddie Hartless and Ronnie Elliott?"

"They're dead!?"

I nodded. I didn't have time for words because another gush of water and an alarming creak of timbers had me glancing up at the ceiling as he struggled to shake off his puzzlement.

"I had no idea. I mean, none of this was in any of the papers."

I tried not to appear put out, but Hebden had a point, a very good

150

point. A local detective and a small-time journalist had both died, but there had been nothing in the papers. Not a word. Not about either of them, or about Fitzsimmons and the girl.

"What about Helen?"

This time Hebden didn't say a word. Maybe it was just the way the light caught him at a certain angle, but I couldn't help thinking he was shaken and deeply hurt.

"I couldn't kill Helen. I couldn't kill anybody!"

"Frankly I find that hard to believe while you're pointing a gun in my face!"

Hebden looked at me and then down at the gun. "It wasn't meant to be this way. I just wanted the stock, but Laughton wouldn't sell."

The timber supports leaned at a crazy angle under the weight of the water above.

Hebden was staring down into the mud. The gun was still in his hand but he looked too lost in thought to use it.

"Hebden, we've got to get out of here!" I yelled, as a cascade of water crashed through the roof bringing down two supporting beams and many of the lights. They crackled, fused and blew, plunging the tunnel into darkness.

I called to Hebden again but he didn't move. I turned and hurried for where I thought the steps should be. A gunshot rang out behind me but I just kept on blindly running, straight into something hard and solid. It snatched at my shoulder and pole-axed me. I crashed to the floor, landing on my back as a huge beam crashed down across my chest and pinned me to the muddy floor. I tried to move but the beam was too heavy and my hand was stuck to the timber. Something had gone straight through the palm of my hand. Only the cold kept me from screaming out.

I lay in the mud and the dark with the water rising around me. I should have let Hebden shoot me. It would have been quicker than drowning. Drowning had to be one of the worst ways to die. It's the sheer inevitability of it, knowing what's going to happen and not being able to do a damn thing about it.

I was going to die and I still had no idea who had killed Eddie Hartless, Ronnie Elliott, Colin and Helen Fitzsimmons, or the mystery girl.

A torch flickered in the distance somewhere to my right. It descended from the sky and moved down towards me. Water swept down over me and filled my lungs. I coughed and choked and spluttered to keep my head above water as a second light appeared.

A dark figure came to a halt above me and a bright light was shone into my face.

"Mahoney? Is that you?"

It sounded like Walker.

"Are you all right?"

I gritted my teeth and managed, "What the hell does it look like?"

Walker ran the light down my body. "Sergeant! Over here. You'd better give me a hand."

I had never thought I'd be pleased to see O'Neal as he crouched down next to Walker and the two of them took hold of the beam.

"Wait," I yelled in agony as my arm was lifted into the air.

"What is it?"

"My hand."

"What about it?"

"I think it's caught on something."

Walker took a look. "Shit!" he mumbled.

"You've got a great bedside manner, Walker!"

He took hold of my hand. "You've got a six-inch nail through the palm of your hand, Mahoney. I'm going to pull it loose, but this is going to hurt."

"Tell me something I don't know."

"Like hell!"

"Here," said O'Neal taking out his truncheon. For one awful minute I thought he was going to beat me unconscious so I wouldn't feel the pain. Instead he held it out to me. "Bite on this."

"Will it make the pain go away?" I asked.

"No, but it'll help keep you quiet!"

He pushed the truncheon into my mouth and I bit down as hard as I could as Walker reached under my fingers and nodded at O'Neal.

"Hold him tight, Sergeant."

My hand inched up. I could feel the nail passing through the flesh, grinding against bone. I bit down with all my might but it didn't do any good. The pain lanced through my body like an axe. Then there was nothing . . .

~

When I came too the rain was still beating down. I was outside, wedged up against the fence. O'Neal was wrapping a sling around my arm. The sleeve of his jacket was torn to shreds. A handkerchief was wrapped around my hand.

"You really ought to speak to your tailor," I quipped.

O'Neal gave a little smile, as if anything else might break his concentration.

"What the hell happened?"

"You passed out."

I tried to move my arm.

"Take it easy, Mahoney. I think it's broken."

We both looked up as Walker emerged from the rubble with Mandy Woodhall draped across his shoulder like a sack of potatoes. He lay her down and draped his coat over her body.

"How is she?" I asked.

"She'll be all right. Just as long as we get an ambulance here quickly."

"I just called for one, it'll be here in a few minutes," replied O'Neal. "I also called the office."

But Walker looked bothered. I turned to see twin beams slip through the darkness as a car came into view. We all looked up to see Superintendent Matthews push a brolly up into the night sky and wade through the mud towards us. He didn't look like he was about to invite anyone for tea.

"What on earth happened here, Walker?"

"We just got here, sir. We found Mahoney and Woodhall down there," he said pointing.

Matthews followed Walker's finger over towards the concrete rubble. He stood silent for a moment and then stepped over to where Mandy was resting. "Is she all right?"

"She caught a bullet, but she'll be fine."

The rain pattered off his umbrella like chips in a frying pan as he turned to glare at me. "And how are you?"

"I've been better!"

"I'm sure you have," he said without affection.

We watched as he kicked his way through the mud towards the rubble. "Anybody else down there?" he asked.

"Only Hebden," Walker replied.

"He got away?"

"I doubt it, sir" said O'Neal. "The whole place collapsed. He's probably been buried alive."

But Matthews was on the warpath. All he needed was a fire and a smear of war paint across his face. His eyes burned a hole deep into O'Neal's skull. "Would you like to put money on that, Sergeant?"

O'Neal swallowed hard and looked at me, then at Walker and at anything and everything else except Matthews.

"What a mess. What a bloody mess!" Matthews sighed.

"Yeah well, maybe if you'd listened to me in the first place, none of his would have happened." I wanted to enjoy the moment. I wanted to bask in the satisfaction of knowing that I'd told them so. It made everything seem worthwhile and I hadn't had a feeling like that in a long time. But the look on their faces as they glanced at one another and then at me, suggested I wasn't about to bask in anything. "What?"

Matthews looked across at Walker. "You haven't told him, have you!?"

Walker was pacing up and down, running a hand through his wet hair. "Told me? Told me what?"

Walker stopped to look at me. His mouth fell open but he didn't say a word. He started to leave. I stood up quickly and stepped out in front of him.

"What is it, Walker? What haven't you told me?"

He looked at me and his eyes said a million things, but nothing I understood. He brushed past me and got into his car.

"Walker!" I yelled. "Walker!"

He started the engine and drove away.

18

The barmaid poured another glass and sat it on the counter in front of me. I took a sip and looked across the empty bar. I was in Spillanes, but there was to be no Summer Breeze to warm my thoughts and no singer to make my toes curl, but the blues hadn't gone away. There was a packet of cigarettes that somebody had left on the counter. I picked it up and thought about lighting one. There was nothing healthy about whisky and cigarettes, but, then again, there was nothing healthy about being a Private Investigator either. It's all sleepless nights, digging around in somebody else's dirt and the rest of the world doesn't even give a damn.

I was halfway through my third glass of whisky when someone placed a carrier bag on the bar next to me. I glanced up to see Walker there loosening his tie.

"What's this?" I asked. "A peace-offering?"

"Actually it's my shopping, but if a loaf of bread and a bar of soap will do, then be my guest!"

I tried not to smile, but it was hard. It was the kind of line I'd have been proud of. Contrary to popular opinion, Walker did have a sense of humour after all. There was hope for the world and everybody in it.

The barmaid stood in front of him and raised her chin like she was half expecting a slap across the face.

"Another two of whatever my friend here's having."

Walker settled on a stool. "Still sore with me, huh?"

"Does it show?"

"I don't blame you of course. I don't blame you at all."

"Is that supposed to make me feel better?"

"Is this?" he replied, handing me a drink.

"It helps."

Walker lit a cigar and blew a ring of smoke up to the low ceiling. A young couple a few stools further down glared at him and moved away, but Walker didn't seem to mind, in fact, he was quite adept at cheesing people off.

"Does it help you to know that you did a great job, Mahoney?"

"No!" I snapped.

"How come?"

I didn't answer.

"I said, how come?"

"Probably because I've spent the last two weeks actually thinking I was doing something worthwhile."

I took a sip of whisky. I didn't hate it any more, not as much as I hated everything else anyway.

"Then you come along and sweep the carpet right from under my feet."

"We had no choice," Walker said, defensively.

"I wouldn't mind so much, but did it never once cross your mind to let me in on your little plan?"

Walker half laughed. "You think we planned all that?"

I looked at Walker and let him know that I damn well thought he had planned it.

He smiled and shook his head. His voice was soft and thoughtful. "As you know, Mandy Woodhall went to Ronnie. She was concerned about the South Cliff area being dangerous so she got him to look around. Unfortunately, around about the same time as all this was going on, his father became very ill and needed twenty-four hour attention . . ."

"So he wasn't dead?"

The Inspector shook his head.

"How can you lie like that?"

He took another drag on his cigar but didn't answer. "Ronnie came to me and said he thought he was on to something. He'd ruffled a few feathers and two goons had started to follow him around. But there wasn't

155

enough for me to warrant spending any time on it."

"So you figured you'd use me!"

Walker stared at me again. "You make it sound so intentional. I had no idea who you were and Ronnie had forgotten all about you turning up. We didn't even know that Helen Fitzsimmons was on to him. That was all down to you, the way you turned it around and began working for her."

I took a sip of whisky and tried not to feel proud of myself, because the last thing I felt right now was proud. Especially with my arm in a sling and my hand all bandaged up. "So you faked Ronnie's death and got me to pick up the pieces?"

"The body we found was a tourist called Ronald Speight. He really had committed suicide."

"And you let me believe . . ." I couldn't go on.

"You'd already convinced yourself that something was going on, you were just having a hard time convincing anybody else."

"You set up Fitzsimmons and the girl and the pictures!"

Walker nodded.

"What was on those negatives anyway?"

The Inspector stubbed out his cigar and shook his head. "I have no idea. It didn't really matter. We just wanted to make you believe somebody had something worth your time."

"You tricked me!"

"It wasn't you we were trying to trick, it was whoever was behind all this."

"You dangled the carrot though, making sure all the bodies and the intrigue kept me interested."

Walker stared at me long and hard. It made me feel uncomfortable.

"Whichever way you want to look at it, you got to who was responsible, and let me tell you, that doesn't happen every time, so I'm grateful."

I sat back on my stool and stared at the glass in my hand. I had to admit, Walker was pretty convincing. So convincing it was growing harder to keep feeling sorry for myself.

"So what about Hebden? Have you found him yet?"

Walker shook his head. "We're hoping to send some people into the tunnels tomorrow. Don't worry, we'll get him, one way or another . . ."

I looked at Walker. "I'm not worried. In fact, there's a part of me that hopes he got away."

The Inspector took a moment to pull out a matchstick and place it between his lips.

"Why's that?"

"Because I'm not sure what he's supposed to have done wrong."

"You mean you've forgotten that somebody died in a hotel because he didn't take care of business and covered everything up?"

"That was an accident and accidents happen."

"It could have been avoided!"

"All he ever wanted was what was best for the town, but all it ever did for him was put him down. He was just trying to save some money. He really liked the place. He wanted to make it into something special, but there were just too many greedy bastards who were in it for themselves. They're the real criminals in all this."

"Is that what you really think?"

"Yeah, that's what I really think."

I finished my drink and picked up my bag. I was ready to head for the door when Walker caught my arm and looked me in the eye.

"We're all guilty of something, Mahoney, it's just that some of us get caught, and some of us don't."

~

The train was due to leave and, with a bit of luck, it might even be on time. I don't know why, but Walker walked with me. Maybe he wanted to make sure I got on the train without leaving any more bodies in my wake for him to clear up. It was raining, hard.

"Does it always rain here?" I asked.

"No, it just feels like it," grunted Walker, hunching his shoulders and running a hand through his wet hair.

I checked the timetable. The train had been delayed by five minutes. I looked down across the cold stone platform and beyond the cold stone walls.

"There's not even a bar here," I groaned.

The Inspector held up a brown paper bag and showed me the whisky bottle inside.

"Here, you never know when it'll come in handy."

We sat on a trolley at the far end of the station and passed the bottle backwards and forwards until a single white light appeared on the track and moved slowly towards us.

I let out a sigh. "You know what hurts me the most?"

"What?"

"The fact that I've never done anything worthwhile in my life, nothing I can be proud of anyway, nothing I can hold my head up and say, I did that."

"And that's how you feel now?"

"Yeah."

"Why?"

"Because I was just playing into your hands. Even Mandy Woodhall was using me."

"You could have walked away any time you wanted to."

"No I couldn't, that's why you kept on about not believing me. Forcing me to go on and discover more and more . . ."

"Actually I didn't like what was going on. It was never my idea. The only reason I went over the top was so you'd get fed up and leave."

I looked at Walker and, as much as I hated to admit it, he appeared to be telling the truth.

"So what are you going to do now?" he asked.

I shrugged my shoulders and took another sip of whisky.

"Go back to Manchester and sign on?"

"Maybe," I mumbled.

"And hope that one day this book of yours sells a million?"

"Just one would do right now."

"You're a fool to yourself, Mahoney, you know that, a bloody fool!"

"I've been called worse!"

"Why don't you stay put?"

"And do what?"

"Ronnie's going to be tied up for some time. He could do with a hand, Mahoney, or Blake or whatever your goddamned name is!"

"I can't."

Walker looked at me as though he wanted to ask why, but he lit another cigar instead. "And what about Trish?" he asked.

"What about her?"

"You like her a lot, don't you?"

I took one last sip of whisky. "I like a lot of women," I said.

The noise of the train's brakes grinding to a halt echoed around the station as weary passengers emerged, carrying heavy suitcases and heavier souls.

I picked up my bag and made for the nearest carriage. Walker followed me to the door.

"You're not going to kiss me goodbye, are you?"

He shook his head and frowned at me.

"What?" I asked.

"I was just thinking."

"About?"

"About how you probably wouldn't have wanted this to end any other way."

"I don't understand."

"You solved the crime but you can't accept the credit. You take a beating for your troubles and you lose the girl. You're a hero, Mahoney, just like in all the best detective novels."

"Is that what you think?"

"You don't care what I think, because if you did you'd stick around."

"Why?" I asked.

"Why?"

"Yeah, why?"

Walker looked at me for a moment as if I was the last clue in his crossword puzzle. He appeared thoughtful, deliberate. He gave the hint that something meaningful was about to shoot from his lips. I was in for a surprise.

"Because," he said.

"Because?"

The Inspector glanced at the floor.

"Is that it? Because! Is that the best you can come up with?"

"What do you want me to do? Beg?"

It was a thought. But as much as I enjoyed the idea of Walker on his knees begging me to stay, I knew it would never happen.

"No. What's the point? You've got your man. End of story."

Walker narrowed his eyes at me.

"You couldn't be more wrong, Mahoney. This isn't just about one man. Finding Hebden, dead or alive, doesn't suddenly make the whole place safe again. There are others like him, doing whatever they can to stay one step ahead of everybody else . . . and that's where you come in."

"Meaning?"

"Meaning the nightmare isn't over, Mahoney. It's only just begun."

THE END

GREAT NORTHERN PUBLISHING
'The home of quality publishing in Yorkshire'

GREAT NORTHERN PUBLISHING is a small, independent, family-owned, multi award-winning company based in Scarborough on the beautiful Yorkshire coast.

We are publishers of paperback books under the Great Northern Publishing imprint; publishers of the well established and much respected magazine, **THE GREAT WAR**, which is dedicated to the First World War 1914-1919; publishers of the highly acclaimed *JADE* adult erotica magazine for men and women, and general mail-order and internet booksellers.

We also specialise in print design and production for a range of clients and individuals. We offer a professional yet personal service, tailored to the needs of individual clients, and pride ourselves on our quality, value, reliability and discretion. We provide a range of competitively costed, quality design and print-based production services for individuals, companies, charities and organisations. Comments and reviews on our products and services, news, awards, examples and detailed information about the company can be found on our easy to navigate website, along with our on-line bookshop and secure ordering facilities.

Orders can also be placed by post, telephone, fax or on-line. You can purchase by credit card, debit card, cheque, postal order, international money order or cash from anywhere in the world.

Our fully illustrated 60-page book, magazine and services catalogue is available FREE from the address below.

This company does not trade under any other name and has no connection or involvement whatsoever with any other company, either here in the UK, or elsewhere, with the same or a similar name, title or business.

ENTERPRISE AWARD

1998 ~ 2000

Great Northern Publishing
PO Box 202, Scarborough, North Yorkshire. YO11 3GE
books@greatnorthernpublishing.co.uk
www.greatnorthernpublishing.co.uk